SIRENS AND SYPHONS

THE EVIE CHESTER FILES: CASE 2

NITA ROUND

Editorial services
KRISTA WALSH

Cover Design
MAY DAWNEY

PINK TEA BOOKS

To readers Everywhere
You are the ones who make this worthwhile

1

E vie Chester wrapped her icy fingers around her cup of tea and stared into the flames of the kitchen stove. Her thoughts were a jumble. Not so long ago, less than three weeks before, she'd been a slave, locked in an old and rundown stable at the back of her owner's property. Beaten, starved, abused, and forced to use her gift to heal anyone who paid. Her life had not been a good one, and she'd believed such was to be her lot in life. Until two women from the Order, a part of Veritas Traders had rescued her.

Freedom hadn't lasted long, though, and her owner, Godwyn Bethwood, had found her. Once caught he'd put her in chains again, and treated her like the slave she was—only worse. Until it all changed, and in some inexplicable twist of fate, she'd regained her freedom for the second time in her life.

This freedom, though, took some getting used to.

In the corner of the room, Agatha Hickman, Evie's landlady and one of the few people she could call a friend, sat in her usual chair with the day's broadsheet spread across her knees.

"It's been two weeks since the Bethwoods released you,

Evie. Are you ever going to leave the house at all?" Agatha asked.

Evie shook her head. "What if it's all a ruse and they capture me again? They call me a Syphon now, whatever that means, and my gifts are too valuable for them to let me go that easily."

"Don't be silly, Evie. Hesta let you go and promised that no one would bother you. You'll never have to deal with the Bethwoods again, not if you don't want to."

"But Hesta might need me again," Evie said. Whenever she thought of Hesta, she couldn't forget the one and only time they'd met. Hesta had been struck mute by the touch of a demon. Evie had not only healed her, but had destroyed the demon.

"She can go to hell after all the trouble they put you through," Agatha said.

"She's a Siren, cursed by demons from hell. I think I'd do pretty much anything to cure myself, too."

"But they bought Gifted slaves as though people can be compared to a prescription from the pharmacy. That is no way to go about curing a problem."

"But—" Evie started.

"No buts Evie, they never had the right to do what they did. To anyone. Those Bethwoods think they own the city." With an impressive amount of noise, Agatha shook the paper and refolded it. "Enough of them. How's Florie doing now that she's not a slave anymore?"

Evie snorted. "She loves her freedom and her work at the theatre. Lighting the lamps and making special effects for the audience appeals to her. She's only a child, after all."

"She's a young woman, or as near as," Agatha said.

"Then she is catching up with the delights of bright lights and fun. More importantly, they welcome her gift as a firestarter."

"Then you should take a leaf out of her book and enjoy your freedom," Agatha said.

"While it lasts?"

"Such a cynic. There are no guarantees for anything in life. Make the most of what you can."

"You're right. Now I'm free I'll need to find some sort of work."

"When Hesta released you, she gave you enough money to be comfortable for several months, Evie. There's no need to fret about that just yet."

"True enough, and Florie is earning her own money at the theatre to pay for her own room. We should be able to manage for a little while."

"That's better. Be positive," Agatha said.

"And thank you for providing us with a home."

Agatha smiled. "My pleasure, but you are both paying your way, so that's no hardship."

"What's going on in the world today?" Evie asked, to change the subject.

"Well. It says that they have found the city governor guilty of corruption, as if we needed a newspaper to tell us that." Agatha shook her head. "Anyway, his position and title are up for the usual political shenanigans. In the docklands, the ship builder Iskabard Speare has landed a contract for thirty small airships. He has a new design for small cargo vessels and now they think he's a hero or something."

"That's a lot of ships, lots of jobs to go around."

"And the headline's a doozy."

"Oh?"

"Yes, indeed," Agatha said. "It says a gifted slave gets to go free after kissing a theatre star."

Evie looked up, and even with the heat of the stove, she could feel her cheeks warming up with embarrassment. "No, it doesn't say that."

"You're right, it doesn't. It says something far more interesting."

"Well, don't keep me guessing!"

Agatha folded the paper so Evie could see the headline and waved it in front of her. "Read it yourself."

At that, Evie sighed. "I can't read."

"I thought not. Do you want to?"

"It would help, probably."

"Then I'll teach you to read. An hour or two every day will be enough, especially since you refuse to go outside."

Evie laughed. She didn't laugh much, but then, the notion that she could express herself without repercussion took time to sink in. "We'll see."

"Anyway, the headlines are unimportant," Agatha said. "The interesting articles are inside and hidden under the corruption stories." She turned the folded paper over in her hand and opened it to the relevant section. "On page nine is a minor piece, no more than a few inches of story, really."

"Well, don't keep me in suspense!" As Evie spoke, a loud knocking at the front door interrupted their discussion.

"Who can that be?" Agatha asked.

"No idea," Evie replied, but she was already on her feet and backing into the corner.

"It's all right, I'll see to it," Agatha said.

In spite of her fears, when Agatha left the room, Evie followed her to the front of the house and watched as she opened the door. A tall man stood outside. He wore a dark suit with a matching cap and a small embroidered badge on his jacket lapel. In his hand he carried three parcels.

"Yes?" Agatha asked.

The man smiled. "Good day to you. I have a delivery for Evie Chester."

Agatha turned around and, at the sight of Evie just a little further down the hallway, she waved her over. "You've got a delivery."

Evie didn't get any closer to the door. "Thank you, leave it at the door."

The man continued to grin as he placed the boxes on the doorstep. He raised his cap, and said, "Many thanks and a good day to you both." He turned away, closed the front gate behind him, and strode off down the street without a second glance.

Agatha grabbed the parcels and dragged them into the house. "Well, give me a hand, Evie. No one is here now."

"But they know."

"They've known ever since young Florie went out to the theatre. Them theatre people don't have the capacity to keep information to themselves."

"You're right, but when they understand what I am, nothing will be the same again," Evie said.

"Worry about that bridge when you get to the river. Meanwhile, give me a hand."

Evie helped Agatha bring the boxes into the kitchen. The boxes weren't that big, but all together they amounted to quite a weight, and even though Evie had used her gifts to make Agatha's old knees feel better, she wasn't that strong. It was too much for Agatha alone.

Evie put the largest box on the table. "Let's see what we have here."

Wrapped in thick brown paper and tied with plenty of sisal string, the first was the size of a shirt box and only a little deeper.

Agatha looked on as Evie cut the wrapping string, carefully removed the wrappings, and opened the box. "Look at these things—a tin of pink tea and a tin of black tea, sugar, cheese crackers, and other food. Well, Evie, someone wants to spoil you. Is there a card or something to say who it is from?"

Evie shook her head. "It's a nice addition to our pantry."

"*Our* pantry?"

"Of course, *our* pantry. I like staying here, and I can't

expect you to supply everything, so this can be my contribution."

"That's not necessary. You pay for board and lodgings, you need not add more."

"Need, no. But I want to," Evie said as she put the box on the floor and turned her attention to the next one. It was half the size of the larger one, slimmer too, and when she opened it, she found a red box with a flip lid. She flipped the lid and looked inside.

Agatha gasped. "Chocolate! Oh my, that's a luxury and a half. A month's wages, at least. I think you have a suitor, Miss Chester. Well, I never. You kept that very quiet."

Heat rose in Evie's cheeks. "I've no idea who sent this. My social circle is mostly slaves, and they'd be hard-pressed to provide a non-stale slice of bread."

Agatha handed Evie the last of her packages. It was much smaller and thinner than the others. "Maybe this one will have a card included," she said.

"Even if it does, that's not much use to me," Evie said.

"Open it up, girl, and let's see what it is. Maybe it'll give you the name of your suitor."

Inside were a couple of items, including a decorative greeting card. She handed that one to Agatha.

"It's a thank-you card."

"Who from?" Evie asked.

"It says, 'Thank you for everything, and most of all thank you for my voice. I'm forever in your debt. If there is anything you need, contact me. Kindest wishes, and I hope we can meet again. Eternally yours, Hesta Estrallia.'" Agatha stared at the card. "It sounds sincere. And she has spent an impressive amount."

"It's just money to them," Evie said. She held in her hand another card. White, and covered with a floral script. She handed that one to Agatha as well.

"Hesta has invited you to afternoon tea at Jacobs Tea House, the finest tea house in all of Bristelle."

"When?"

"Tomorrow at two of the clock," Agatha said. "Will you go?"

"I'm not sure. What do you think?"

"I think you might like to see what she has to say. If she'd intended any trouble, she'd have done it already. After all, it would be easier here than at such a fine tea house where people could see."

2

_____

Of all the tea houses in the city, Jacobs Tea House on Great Herman Street had the biggest front window that Evie had ever seen. Located in the Salverton district of Bristelle city, Jacobs was a part of what would once have been a part of the great hall until they'd separated it all off into smaller dwellings, offices, and shops. Jacobs Tea House itself filled what would have been the entrance hall to this building. And what a grand hall it had been.

Inside, two carved stone stairways on either side of the room swept around to a balustraded landing that joined them together. It offered a grand view, too, of all the tables and people inside the tea house. Behind the balustrade, a broad corridor led deeper into the building.

On the ground floor, at the back of the hall, double doors led into the kitchens, or at least, Evie supposed they did. An impressive number of waiters strode purposefully through the doors with trays in their hands. Each one of them wore a black suit with a plain black waistcoat and their shirts starched brilliant white. They all wore white gloves, too, for fear of contaminating the utensils, she supposed.

When she walked through the doorway into the room

proper, she'd not gone more than three steps before a snooty waiter stopped her from going any further. He eyed her clothing from head to foot and pursed his lips with disapproval.

"Excuse me," he said, in a way that suggested anything but.

"You are excused," Evie said, and she glanced around the room to see if Hesta had arrived.

"You misunderstand," he continued. "This is a fine establishment, and we are very particular–"

"I'm sure you are," Evie interrupted. "But I'm expected."

"I see."

The door swung open behind her, but Evie didn't react. Instead she stared at the waiter.

"And who would be expecting *you*?" he asked, with an emphasis that Evie did not care for.

Before she could speak, a feminine voice said, "That would be me, Arthur."

He bowed. "Of course, of course."

Hesta stepped around Evie. She looked perfect. Her dark hair had been delicately coiffured, and she had a twinkle in her dark eyes. "This is Evie Chester, Arthur. Please be nice. She is going to be one of the most influential people in all of Bristelle."

Arthur looked Evie up and down once more. "As madam wishes." He started to walk towards the rear of the room. "A table this way?

Hesta turned to Evie. "Where would you like to sit, Evie?"

Evie pointed to an empty table near the window. "There," she said. "I want to look at the people as they walk by."

"Excellent," Hesta said. "We'll take that one there, please, Arthur, and we'd like your finest afternoon tea. If that's all right with you, Evie?"

"Of course, whatever you want."

Hesta led Evie to the table. "What I want is for you to be happy. That's what I want most of all," she said.

"Seriously?"

"Can I take your coats, ladies?" Arthur asked.

Evie removed her coat, and Arthur took it with his disdain barely concealed. He held her clothing in his hands as though terrified he would catch poverty or something equally as heinous. Hesta threw her coat over his arm. "Tea, Arthur. We'll start with the Mahgran Green."

"Very good, madam. Excellent choice."

Evie waited for him to walk out of earshot before she spoke. "Are you trying to impress me?"

"Yes," Hesta said.

"I can't be bought like that."

"I know that. This is just tea, Evie. Nothing more."

Evie cocked her head to the side and regarded Hesta with narrowed eyes. "With the Bethwoods, nothing is that simple."

"Never mind. Just enjoy the tea," Hesta said.

Evie sat where she had the best view of the street. They were in the richest part of Bristelle, and there were no common workers on these streets. Even the shop girls wore clothing she could never hope to have.

"I'm glad you came," Hesta said.

"It's a bit swanky for the likes of me, and I don't think Arthur cares for me much."

"That's Arthur. People here like him even though he looks down his nose at everyone."

Evie snorted. "He's pretentious."

Hesta removed her gloves and laid them on the seat next to her. "He also owns this place. His prices are prohibitive for many, and only the rich and important dare enter."

"And you asked me, a slave–"

"Ex-slave, Evie, and you have no marks of ownership. You're a free woman."

"A poor free woman."

"Free and important," Hesta replied.

"Excuse me," Arthur interrupted them. Evie glared at him. He'd moved so quietly she hadn't heard him approach. "Mahgran Green Tea, first flush from the easternmost slopes of Mount Panrham." He placed a small teapot and two tiny cups with saucers on the table.

Evie stared at the brightly painted set, which, in her mind, looked child sized. He placed a small egg timer in an ornate silver holder beside the teapot. Half of the sand had run through. "Excuse my ignorance, but what is a first flush?

Arthur stared over the table as though about to give a grand lecture on teas. "The first flush is when the freshest young leaves and buds are picked. On occasion, we also have the first tea, which is the very first batch of the season. Some say the newest buds have the greatest flavour."

"And do they?" Evie asked.

"It would depend on the tea and the growers," he replied.

"Excellent, thank you, Arthur. Give us time to drink this, and then we'll have a full spread with Winchor Black Tea, if you don't mind," Hesta said.

"As you wish." He inclined his head in a half-hearted bow.

"One more thing, if you have the newspapers, I would appreciate it."

"The Bristelle Echo or the Mid-Angle Times?" he asked.

"Both."

"Of course, madam." Then he moved away as silently as he had arrived.

"He's creepy," Evie said. "How does anyone move that quietly?"

"Practice, I suspect. I hope you don't mind that I took care of the tea order?"

Evie shook her head. "Except I'm not sure that I can afford these prices. What are the prices?"

"Arthur has a rule— if you need to ask, you can't afford it."

Evie snorted.

"Don't worry. My treat. But if it makes you feel better, I'll add the bill to my brother's account."

Evie couldn't stop the smile that threatened. The idea that Godwyn Bethwood, her old owner, would pay her tea bill seemed fitting somehow. She wished she could make him pay a lot more. "So to what do I owe the pleasure of your invitation?"

"Shall I pour?" Hesta asked.

Evie waved her hand over the table. "Feel free, you're in charge."

Hesta frowned as she poured the tea into the cups. "It's a subtle flavour, so best drunk without milk, sugar, or honey. Is that all right with you?"

"I've never had green tea, so I bow to your superior knowledge," Evie answered.

The frown on Hesta's face deepened. She lifted her cup and took a deep breath to take in the aroma of the tea.

"Are all the cups and teapots child size here?"

Hesta chuckled. "No, only the green tea. It's just a little light refreshment before we eat."

"So, why am I here?"

"Did you like your gifts?"

"You're evading my question, but yes, thank you. It was a nice gesture."

Hesta gazed into her eyes for a moment, then looked away. "I wanted to see you."

"Why?"

"Great Mother of all creation, you don't make things easy, do you?"

"Should I?"

Hesta paused before she sipped at her tea and regarded

Evie over the rim of her tea cup. "Because you have been on my mind since the day we met."

Once more, Evie could feel the rise of heat in her cheeks.

Hesta replaced her cup in the saucer. "And part of me wants to make up for all we've done to you."

Evie took a small sip of her tea. It was nice and light. Pleasant even. "And what about all the other slaves Godwyn used and abused?"

"I can't do anything about the past, Evie."

"But what about the future?"

"I shall try to do better. Godwyn, too," Hesta said.

"I'll believe that when I see it happen. In fact, I will believe that when he does something to benefit those worse off than he is."

Hesta smiled and drank her tea. Evie couldn't help but stare at her. Beautiful as ever. Famous. Rich. But the question that overwhelmed Evie most of all was why did she really want Evie with her?

In the silence that followed, Arthur and two other waiters wheeled a trolley by the side of the table. On the top, there were tiny triangles of so many types of sandwiches Evie's mouth dropped open. Then there were the cakes: small cakes, larger cakes, slices of different and varied gateaux with chocolates and creams, fresh fruit, and compotes. Evie's mouth watered at the sight of it all.

When she tore her gaze from the display, she saw Hesta looking at her. For a moment, she looked open and unguarded, and Evie saw in those dark eyes a twinkle of simple delight.

Arthur replaced the tiny teapot with a normal sized one, and fresh cups and saucers. This time he provided a milk jug and sugar bowl. He placed the newspapers on the table at Hesta's side.

"Thank you, Arthur. I'll take it from here."

"Yes, ma'am."

Evie filled her small plate with a pile of sandwiches, one of every type, and she stared at them as Hesta poured tea.

"Eat," Hesta said. "As much as you want."

Evie grinned at the thought of all the food. Once eaten, no one could take it away from her. She picked up a small crustless triangle and paused with the sandwich halfway to her mouth. "What will it cost me?" she asked.

She didn't wait for the answer but bit into the sandwich, chewed, and swallowed. In the last two weeks, she'd become used to regular food, so this bounty wouldn't mean that she'd lose control of herself. She would probably eat too much, though, because she remembered in the back of her mind the many years of privation. She decided to put a few cakes in her bag for Florie.

"There is no cost. Unless being in my company is unpleasant to you?"

Evie shook her head and ate more of her food. After that, she refused to speak until her plate had been cleared.

"Cake? What would you like?" Hesta asked.

"All of them," Evie replied. She stared at Hesta to see her response. Hesta laughed and then filled Evie's plate with a selection of small pastries. Evie first selected a choux finger topped with chocolate and filled with cream. She ate that one in two bites, and all the while Hesta watched her eat. When she'd had enough, she slowed down. She sipped her tea and nibbled on a small sugarcoated pastry. A smile lifted the corners of her mouth.

"What are you smirking at?"

"Life," Evie answered. After years of being a slave and hidden away, it tickled her to be able to sit in the open surrounded by people who'd never even noticed her existence. Best of all, she was the one eating posh cake and drinking expensive tea.

Hesta opened the papers. "Have you read the news?"

Evie sat back in her seat, her shoulders and back straight

and still. She regarded Hesta with narrowed eyes. "I was a slave, Hesta Bethwood. No one bothered to teach me things such as reading, writing, or counting."

Undaunted, Hesta pulled the broadsheets in front of her. "Godwyn wishes to move into politics, and there's a new position that's just opened up."

"The city governor," Evie said.

"I thought you didn't read?"

"I don't, but my friend and landlady does. She keeps me informed."

"Anyway, yes, you're right, that's the one. Godwyn has a lot of power in the city now. He could move up in the world."

"Would that power be as a result of healing the right people?"

Hesta nodded. "In part, yes."

"And what has that got to do with me? He could hang by the neck, for all I care."

"He wants to set up a place for the gifted. Maybe an academy, or something like the Towers of Knaresville, but in Bristelle."

"Hell, no," Evie responded.

"Let me read from the papers. Godwyn says, 'Long have the gifted of Bristelle been abused and misused. The gifted are in possession of skills that should be encouraged for the benefit of all. I want to change the way we consider these people, so that those with gifts can contribute to the city without fear of recrimination. To do this, I would like the city to set up an institute for the gifted, an academy for all people to meet and allow their gifts to be used. If they need to make a living using their gifts, then that is only fair. After all, you wouldn't expect a carpenter to create a table for free, now would you?' He says that in the *Echo*."

"Bloody hell," Evie said. "He's changed his tune."

"Perhaps now that he's fully aware of my gifts, and I've been healed, his attitude has changed as a result."

"Attitudes and actions don't change that much, nor so fast."

Hesta tilted her head to one side and regarded Evie with a steady gaze. "Not really. He has always known of the gifted."

"He's used us enough."

"And most important of all, Godwyn always looks after his family."

"I'd say so."

"He would like you to be a part of this institute."

"Again, hell, no. Not even if he swore an oath in front of every person in the whole of Bristelle. I wouldn't trust him as far as I could spit fire."

"What about if I did?"

"If you did what? Swear an oath? Or maybe you can spit fire?"

Hesta looked at her with a most determined expression on her face. "If I set up an institute, would you help me?"

Speechless, Evie leaned back in her seat. She hadn't realised until then that she had started to lean forward.

"Would you, Evie? Would you join me in this venture to bring the gifted into the public with rights and protections like they have never had before in Bristelle?"

Evie didn't know what to say. In her mind, Hesta's voice said, *'Please, I need your strength and will to make a difference and to make up for what we've done to you and the others.'*

'Don't speak into my head like that,' Evie immediately replied. Out loud she said, "Why now?"

"In truth, I've been trying for years, but I couldn't get it established. I had no voice, and Godwyn had money and no power."

"But why were you even trying?"

"Because I believe in having a place, and it would have meant that we could hear more about healers."

"So it was all about you?"

"You make me sound quite cold and calculating."

"Not really." She stared at Hesta through narrowed eyes. "You were desperate. I was there when I cured you, remember. I saw your reaction, and that was not the reaction of someone cold and calculating."

"Thank you." Hesta looked away. "You gave me hope. And now, I think we can do more for others."

"Perhaps." Evie folded her arms across her chest. "I'll think about it."

3

_____

E vie sat with Agatha and Florie at the table in the kitchen. They'd finished eating dinner, and Evie could feel a smile of contentment cross her face. She felt safe, finally, and in the company of the two people who meant the most to her. She wondered if Hesta would feel as comfortable here, or if Agatha would like her.

"Are you going to do that school thing with Hesta Estrallia then?" Florie asked.

"It's Hesta Bethwood, and don't you forget it," Evie answered.

"But Evie–"

"No buts, Florie. You know very well our history and where we came from."

Florie shoved a piece of chocolate into her mouth and chewed defiantly. "She buys you nice things, Evie. Why is that?"

"None of your business, you cheeky money," Evie answered.

Agatha crossed her cutlery on her plate and wiped her mouth. "It's a good question, though. Are you going to be involved with the place they want to create?"

Evie shrugged. "I don't know. It sounds like a good idea, and it'd be good to help other gifted people in Bristelle. Not everyone can go to the Towers of Knaresville."

"Just be careful. After all, it's the Bethwoods, and I wouldn't trust either of them," Agatha said.

Evie wiped her mouth once she'd finished eating. "I'll consider it is a little more when I have the time. Right now, there are more pressing problems."

"Such as?" Agatha asked.

"I need to sort out an income. When I have money coming in, then I think I'll be able to help make life a little easier on the gifted."

"That's sensible."

"If I do anything with the Bethwoods, I'd appreciate your advice, Agatha."

"Of course. But I'm surprised you want to have anything to do with them."

Evie shrugged.

"In that case, make sure you are protected legally. And if there is any paperwork of the legal sort, I know just the man to look at it," Agatha said.

Evie smiled. She seemed to do that rather more these days. She wondered what it would be like when she had really adjusted to freedom. Would she smile more? Would she laugh? "We'll see."

"When I go to work tomorrow, I could speak with Miss Estrallia and tell her you want to talk about things."

Miss Estrallia? Evie thought.

"She is very easy to talk to, you know," Florie continued. "And–"

"I think Florie has a bad case of hero worship," Agatha said.

"Has she indeed," Evie replied. "I better have a word with Miss *Estrallia* about that."

Florie almost bounced in her seat. "I'll tell her. I'll tell her first thing. Promise I will. Is it all right if I go and see Simple?"

Now Evie did manage a quiet chuckle. "You're still seeing that lad, Simple Simon? I hope he's not teaching you any more bad habits, like how to pinch things?"

Florie shook her head. "No, Evie. There's no need now we get food every day." She smiled at Agatha. "And good food, too."

"Off you go," Agatha said. "But don't come back late. And if you want to carry on seeing this young man, then perhaps you'd better invite him here so we get to meet him. We have to make sure he is suitable for you."

"He should come for tea on Sunday afternoon," Evie said.

"Yes, yes," Florie said as she raced out of the room. The front door slammed closed behind her.

"Bless her," Agatha said. "You did good, Evie. She's adjusting very well. You wouldn't know the things she's been through from the look of her now."

"She's like my little sister, and if I did one good thing, then setting Florie free would be it." Evie fiddled with the edge of her plate.

"Is there something bothering you?"

"What do you think of this institute idea?" Evie asked.

Agatha took a moment to think of her response. "On the whole, I think it's a good idea. We could do with something like that in Bristelle. It just needs the right people in control to make sure that it is not abused, and that the people who go there are protected. Being gifted is an honour given by the Mother, but not everyone sees it that way. You know that as well as any one does."

"I do," Evie agreed. "I'd like to see what Hesta has to say about it all, though. That might make a difference."

No matter her words, she wasn't at all sure that anything would come of it. At the back of her mind was the thought

that the idea had originated with Godwyn, and he cared for
no one but himself.

4

_____

After lunch, the pile of dishes in the sink had mounted up. Agatha was out, Florie was at work, and it was time to clean up not just the sink, but the parlour. Evie boiled water on the stove and added it to the corner sink. She'd just made a start on the dishes when she heard a knock at the front door.

She was all alone. Should she answer it, or ignore it?

Evie dried her hands whilst she decided what to do, and then the person at the door knocked again. She made her way to the front of the house and looked out through a small window into the street.

Hesta stood no more than two feet away. She wore a simple dress and a long cream scarf wrapped around her neck—a reminder that although Evie had removed the curse that had taken away Hesta's voice, she could do nothing about the ragged scars that devastated her skin.

With a deep breath for courage, Evie opened the door just as Hesta prepared to knock again.

"Good afternoon, Evie," Hesta said. "I hope this is not too inconvenient a time to call?" She adjusted the long leather straps of her purse bag so that it hung closer to her side and held up a small cardstock box tied with a string to stop the lid from opening. "I've brought a selection of cakes for you. I thought we could sit and talk over tea." When Evie didn't answer straight away, she added, "Florie said it would be all right." She smiled, but it was tentative and unsure.

Evie stared at the woman. "Hesta, as you can see, I'm not dressed for company." When Hesta didn't respond, Evie shrugged. "I don't suppose it matters much, you've seen me dressed in worse." She took a step back and allowed Hesta the space to enter. "Come in. I'll make a pot of tea."

"Thank you."

Evie didn't know what to make of Hesta's presence. She wondered, too, if she should make one of the fancy teas that she'd sent in her parcel. Maybe she wouldn't like the cheap black they used every day. If she wanted to be vindictive, she could use stewed tea, but no matter how tempting the thought, she wasn't sure if she could be that petty.

Evie paused as she opened the pantry cupboard. "Did you send the teas so you would have something fancy to drink should you wish to visit?"

"I sent those for you. I'm happy drinking whatever you want to drink."

"Then everyday black it is. Nothing fancy."

Evie made a pot of tea, and they sat at the table as they waited for the leaves to steep. Silence filled the kitchen.

Evie poured out the tea into two white cups. These were the everyday cups. The glaze had cracked, and fine discoloured lines crisscrossed the insides from the bottom to the top. They weren't the best that Agatha owned, but Evie had no right to use what wasn't hers and she wasn't about to apologise for it.

She pushed one of the cups towards Hesta. "Help yourself to milk and sugar."

"Thank you." Hesta pulled the cup closer to her and

added a little milk. Then she sat back in her seat and regarded Evie with her dark and unreadable eyes. "Evie?"

Evie pulled her shoulders back and closed her eyes. She took a couple of deep breaths to settle herself. "What is it you want from me? Why are you here?"

"I thought it was obvious."

"No."

"I came to see you," Hesta said. "But do you even want me here?" She reached out to touch Evie's hand.

Evie couldn't help it; she flinched away, and Hesta withdrew her hand as though burned.

"Florie said…" And then Hesta's words faded away.

"I don't know what I want right now, and Florie says lots of things, not all of them right," Evie said, and opened her eyes. "I should hate you."

"And do you?"

"No. I don't. With all that has happened, I should hate the world, but I don't. I'm not sure I trust you, though, not with your brother and everything."

Hesta nodded.

"Florie's different. She's young, and she has a big case of hero worship. She thinks you could walk on water if you wanted."

"But not you?"

"You've charmed her, for sure," Evie said.

Hesta put her cup down so fast and hard that tea sloshed over the side and dripped down to the table. "Is that what you think I've done to her? Charmed her with my voice?"

"You're a siren, that's what you do. Men, women, whoever you want to do something for you."

Hesta sat back in her seat and closed her eyes. "I'm sorry you think that of me." When she opened her eyes, she gazed at Evie for several moments before she spoke. "I don't blame you, of course, and I know it'll take a while to trust me. But I promise, I truly promise, to earn your trust if you'll let me."

"It might take a while."

"As long as it takes. Don't give up on me, Evie Chester."

"Why is this important?"

Hesta smiled enigmatically. "It just is."

At that the front door opened and slammed shut. "Evie, are you in?" Agatha called out.

"In the kitchen," Evie replied.

"Put the kettle on, love," Agatha called back. "I'm parched. Just let me hang my coat first."

The door to the hallway cupboard opened and closed, and finally Agatha walked into the kitchen. "Do you want a…" She stopped.

Hesta rose to her feet and held out her hand. "I'm Hesta Estrallia, from the theatre," she said. "Pleased to make your acquaintance."

Agatha stared at the proffered hand, then shook it. "Good day to you, Hesta *Bethwood*. You can call me Mrs. Hickman. How is your brother these days?"

Hesta and Agatha stared at each other, and Evie thought it quite possible they would come to blows. Then Hesta smiled, "My brother is my brother and does as he pleases. But I'm very pleased to meet you. I can tell you are just the sort of woman to provide a good and stable home for Florie. And Evie, of course."

"Of course," Agatha said.

"Tea, Agatha?" Evie asked. "Let me just add a little more hot water to the pot."

Hesta move the box of cakes into the center of the table. "Cakes would go well, don't you think, Mrs. Hickman?"

Agatha pulled up a chair and sat almost next to Evie. "That would be lovely, yes."

Evie placed a fresh cup before Agatha and filled it with tea.

"Thank you, dear," Agatha said. "But business, I think, first. Have you both discussed this institute, or academy, tower, or whatever you choose to call it? What did you decide?"

Evie shook her head. "We've not discussed anything yet."

"I think, if you're going to get involved with the Bethwoods, then you need to know exactly what it is all about," Agatha said, as though Hesta was not there. "All of it. And you'll also want to know if, and what, you'll be paid, and how much protection you'll be given should things not go well or if there is an unexpected turn of events."

"What sort of thing do you mean by unexpected, Mrs. Hickman?"

"Well, unexpected things wouldn't be unexpected if I knew what they were in advance, now, would they?"

Hesta chuckled softly to herself. "Of course not."

"Anyway, we haven't gotten that far," Evie said.

"Now that you mention these things, I have something for you." Hesta reached inside her bag and pulled out a small sheaf of papers. "I came prepared," she said, and unfolded the papers on the table.

"You know I can't read these," Evie said.

"I know. I wanted to give them to you and suggest that you get a legal representative. But Mrs. Hickman here is a very practical woman, she'll know who you can see. If I give you these now, then you can think over all of the proposals."

Agatha nodded her head once. "Very good. I like that you are ready and have given thought to Evie."

"Always. My family has not been good to her. I would like to make recompense."

"Fine, but I think you'd better tell us what you have in mind to achieve this recompense," Agatha said.

"It's in the details here." Hesta gestured to the papers she had provided. "It's a simple idea. I believe there should be a place in Bristelle for the gifted, like the Towers in Knaresville."

"But the towers have magic within their walls," Agatha said.

"Yes, they do. And eventually, we could perhaps build a tower. Even without the earth magic to fill it, it would still represent most clearly what we are about."

"And what is that?" Evie asked.

Hesta turned her attention to Evie. "A safe place for the gifted to get help, or to be themselves. A place where mundanes might be able to hire the services of the gifted without fear. We can protect each other. Protect the gifted from outsiders and protect the non-gifted from the powers of the gifted. We can build up a good working relationship given time, and that would benefit us all."

"Then why haven't you done that already?" Agatha asked. "Why now?"

Hesta turned her full attention to Agatha. "Do you think this is just a whim of mine?"

"Yes," Agatha said.

Hesta stared at Agatha for a moment and nodded once. "Evie asked me the same question when we went for tea. I understand your reluctance to see anything but ill from me… from us. I shall say that we have tried to get this set up many times, but there has been much resistance. There is a feeling that if you want to see the gifted, then you must go to the towers only."

"You don't agree?" Agatha asked.

"No, I don't. We have gifts, and no matter what they are, we should use them to help others. And help people here, not in some other city that cares nothing for us."

"Like you helped me and others?" Evie asked. "By putting us into slavery?"

"That was not my idea." Hesta looked away. "It was an idea that ran away from us, and when Godwyn couldn't fix my problem, his approach became increasingly more extreme."

"And you did nothing about it," Agatha said.

"I'm sorry." Hesta rested her hands in her lap and stared at her entwined fingers.

Agatha grunted and topped up her tea cup. "Better late than never at all, I suppose."

"I should have known what was going on, but I didn't. I didn't want to know, if I'm honest. I just wanted to be well again."

Agatha placed the teapot on the table with an indelicate thud.

"I'm well now. I must repay Evie and people like her. There is so much more I can do," Hesta continued. Her voice sounded tentative, and she chewed at her lower lip.

"A tower, you say," Agatha said.

"A tower to inspire trust."

At that, Evie snorted.

"Seriously. Ordinary people don't trust the gifted. They're scared of them," Hesta said.

"Scared of *us*, you mean," Evie corrected.

"Yes," Hesta admitted. "We have magic they don't understand, and they hate us for it."

"You must also never forget that there some known to abuse their gifts," Agatha added.

"Such as making people do things they might otherwise not," Evie said.

Hesta sighed. "You'll never forgive me, will you?"

Evie stood up. "I didn't say that. Never is such a long time, but it will take more than five minutes of pretty talking."

Hesta looked down at her hands again. They were clasped so tightly together that her knuckles and fingers were white. In that moment, Evie's hardness lessened. "Show me your neck. Let me see how it's doing," she said.

"It's fine. The scars will never go away. But I can talk now, and I have you to thank for it."

"Show me," Evie demanded.

"Here?"

"Yes, right here, right now."

Hesta unwrapped the scarf and draped it over the back of her seat. Agatha's sharp intake of breath meant that she had also seen the ravaged skin of her throat.

"Oh, you poor love," Agatha said.

"Let me see," Evie said. She closed her eyes and tried to focus her thoughts. When she opened them, she saw such hope within the depths of Hesta's brown eyes that she felt herself soften with concern.

"Does it hurt?" she asked.

"Not really. It's stiff and hard, but it doesn't stop my voice."

"I'm going to touch the scars. Is that all right?"

Hesta swallowed hard. "Yes," she whispered.

"If I hurt you, tell me, and I'll stop."

Hesta nodded, and Evie reached out and touched the worst of the scars with the tips of her fingers. The rough and ridged skin, puckered and melted from the unnatural heat of a demon's hand, had lost all semblance to normal soft skin.

"I'm so sorry," Evie said. Her hand brushed across the ridges, and although she couldn't see any unnatural darkness in the tone, something didn't feel right.

A tingle at the tips of her fingers forewarned her of a change. Her gift responded to the sense of wrongness, and as she lightly pressed against Hesta's neck, she could just see the lost embers of the demon's touch, like tiny glittering speckles of the curse. She'd killed the demon, banished him from the earth, and his curse had died with him. Only the devastating effects of his touch on Hesta's skin remained.

"Stay still," Evie said, and she called to these small remnants. A warmth flowed through her fingers, and a buzz settled in every muscle. She found herself aglow. The remnants flowed into her slowly, and the more they flowed, the more she understood the working of the curse and the more enlivened she felt.

Her heart boomed against her ribs, and she knew that her chest heaved as though she'd run a great distance. Beneath her hands, the blood in Hesta's neck pulsed faster and harder.

Hesta moaned, and Evie pulled away as though burned.

"Are you all right?" Evie asked.

Hesta stared up at her, and her brown eyes were almost black. "Do you know what this is like?" she asked, her voice low and husky.

Evie shook her head. "Does it hurt that bad?"

"The very opposite," she answered. "You better stop before I..." She let the words drift away.

"Before you what?" Evie asked.

Behind her, Agatha coughed. A delicate little attention-getting cough. "I think she's saying that she is very tired, aren't you, dear?"

Hesta nodded with great enthusiasm. "Yes. Yes, that would be it."

Evie stepped back and stared at Hesta's throat. "That helps a little, I think. I'll do a little more when you are less tired." Then she wrapped Hesta's neck with the scarf. "Small steps, then. A bit at a time."

"Dear Mother, you're going to kill me."

"Oh, I hope not," Evie said, seriously. "That would not be a good outcome at all." She stared at Hesta's neck. "I can make a difference here, but I need to look into this more. If I knew more about my gift, then perhaps I'd be better at this."

Hesta took several deep breaths, and when she spoke she sounded out of breath. "Then maybe we should try and discover more about your gift."

"We?"

"I know many people. Maybe someone will know something helpful. I'd like to help, if I can."

Evie didn't need to think about that for long. "Yes, I would appreciate your help." She sat down and took a sip of her cool tea. "I need to know who I am. Or maybe I should say, what I am."

Hesta reached out and gripped Evie's hand. "Let me show you something."

"What? When?"

"Now. Come out with me. I want you to see what I have done so far." Then she smiled. "Unless you need to purge?"

Evie nodded. Both of them had seen her purge before, and there seemed little point in hiding it. Even if she wasn't full yet, there was no point holding on to it.

She stood at the sink with her back to Agatha and Hesta, and pushed all of the deadness from Hesta out through the edges of her finger nails. As the skin split, she gritted her teeth against the pain. Drops of grey ooze, rather than the usual black, seeped from under her skin and dropped into the sink. The rancid stench of corruption filled her mouth. She spat out the vile slime that coated her taste buds and then waited for the purge to stop. It didn't take long, and as soon as she had finished, the rips along her nails had healed and stopped stinging so much.

Evie took a mouth full of cold tea from her cup, swished it around to clear away the residual taste of the purge, and spat it into the sink.

"I'm done," she said.

5

E vie didn't often go outside the house unless she had to. Now, she walked down Ardmore Street as though she did it every day. She was with Hesta, so nothing bad could happen.

As though to reinforce that thought, Hesta linked arms with Evie, and they walked down the street as though they'd been friends for years.

"Where are we going?" Evie asked.

"Not far," Hesta replied.

They walked to the corner of Pump Street, and Hesta stopped near the entrance to the Gin Palace. She stood at the edge of the path and held out her hand until a small two-wheeled calash stopped next to her. The soft collapsible roof remained upright, and Hesta opened the short door and they got inside.

"Mistress Bethwood," the driver said, and tipped his cap.

"Good day to you, thank you for waiting," she said.

"Always a pleasure. Can't complain about waiting. Not on such a fine day. The weather is good and dry, although rain later, so they say. But I'll be home by then."

Evie stared at Hesta. She couldn't believe that Hesta could

make small talk with ordinary people. "I didn't know you had a carriage."

"I don't. But I've travelled with Charlie many times."

"He was waiting for you, then?" Evie asked.

"Yes. I try to hire him whenever I can."

Charlie leaned back in his seat. "And I like to drive for Miss Bethwood. Which is why I always hang about the theatre for my fares, in case she needs me. Things will change now, I think."

"And I appreciate it very much," Hesta said.

"Where to, ma'am? The new place, is it?"

"Yes, please, straight there."

"Sit tight," he said. He clicked his tongue and off they moved.

"We're going to your new place? I don't understand."

"I've been looking at taking a new direction for quite some while. Meeting you seems to have pushed things forward. You'll see."

Evie kept her thoughts and questions to herself as they clattered through Ardmore, Cainstown, and headed towards the finer end of Bristelle. They passed the fine shops of Salverton in the west and Evie recognised the road that led to Jacobs Tea House. They went a little further alongside the Vyon river, but stopped just before they reached the bridge. The houses here were larger than the ones in Ardmore, with more space between them.

Hesta opened the carriage door and jumped out onto the pavement. She held out her hand for Evie to take. "Come on, let me show you around."

Evie looked at Hesta's offered hand and hesitated for only a few seconds. With a gift like hers, touching another person wasn't always a pleasant experience. She ignored her offered assistance and jumped down herself.

Hesta lowered her hand and wiped it over her skirt. "I'm clean."

Evie didn't respond.

The three-storey red brick building had a ten-foot brick and wrought iron fence along the front. It didn't look like a normal house but more industrial, and without much ornamentation of the brickwork it could very well have been a set of offices.

To one side, she could see a set of gates that led to the coach house, but they didn't stop near them. They'd stopped near an impressive and ornate gateway that allowed access to the building. A cobbled pathway, culminating in a shallow step covered with pretty tiles laid out in a colourful geometric design, led to the porch, which was open sided with a hipped slate roof.

The front door, painted a deep and glossy black, had a large brass knocker set in the middle of the door level with Evie's eyes. On the walls to both sides of the door were two small windows to allow a little light into the hallway.

"Here we are. What do you think?" Hesta asked.

"It's big."

Hesta pulled a bundle of keys from her bag. The first key failed to open the lock. As did the second key. On the third attempt, the door opened from the inside, and Godwyn Bethwood stood on the threshold of the house.

Bethwood!

Fear took her breath away. Her heart pounded and her knees almost gave way as she tried to back up. Bethwood, the monster who'd kept her imprisoned, kept her as a slave, and treated her worse than if she'd been livestock.

"Hello, Hesta. I did not expect you just yet." He looked at Evie. "And our Evie, how wonderful. Is she going to help you after all?"

"What?" Evie almost squeaked. She turned to run, but Hesta grabbed her arm.

"Don't run, please. Stay," Hesta said. "And Godwyn, stop trying to act so terrifying."

"Trying?" Evie said. "He doesn't have to try."

"I'm trying nothing," he said, and grunted. "On my best behaviour, as I promised."

"Still scary," Evie said.

"There's no need to be scared. Come on in." He stepped backwards and waved them into the hallway.

Evie didn't know whether to walk inside or run away. She thought of her chances of getting far, and as she considered her options, Hesta ushered her into a huge wood-paneled reception hallway. The hallway was so grand and large it stretched into the bowels of the house. Black and white tiles in a chequered pattern covered the floor, and each one was spotless. A small jardinière sat in the corner with some broad leafed thing that Evie didn't recognise.

Godwyn stepped further into the hallway.

There were doors opposite the staircase and a couple at the far end. Evie eyed those doors as though she expected Mr Grobber to join them. Hesta closed the front door with a slam and Evie flinched at the finality of the sound.

"Shall I make tea first, then you can have the tour?" Godwyn asked. He seemed totally oblivious to Evie's discomfort.

"Good idea," Hesta said.

"I'm not so sure..." Evie started. She tried to remain calm, but she couldn't help herself from trying to sidle closer to the exit.

Hesta flipped her around and grabbed both arms. "Please, Evie. I don't want you to be alarmed."

Evie looked down at the hands holding her arms. Fear gave way to anger. "Forcing me to stay is not going to help much."

Hesta let her go and stared down at the floor. "I'm so sorry. I could sense your panic, and this was the first... the second option I could think of."

"Second?"

"I would have sung you calm, but that would have been an affront to you," Hesta said.

"Yes. That would have been the very last thing you ever said to me."

"That's what I thought. Truly, I'm sorry. I didn't mean to try and restrain you in that way."

"In what way did you wish to restrain me, then?"

"I just... I just wanted to stop you from running away. Nothing will harm you here."

"The door is there." Evie pointed so that there could be no confusion. "I could leave right now?"

Hesta took a couple of steps to the side so that Evie had a clear way out. "Yes, I'm sorry. If you wish to go, then I wouldn't stop you. I would be very disappointed, though."

"Well–" Evie started, but Godwyn interrupted her.

"So are you staying for tea, Evie?"

It took Evie a moment or two to process the question. "What?"

"I'll go and make some, shall I?" With that, Godwyn turned around and opened one of the doors at the far end of the building. As fast as the door closed behind him, it opened again. "Do you want tea cakes or biscuits with that?" he asked.

"Both," Hesta said without turning around, her eyes fixed firmly on Evie.

"Maybe you should show her the library," he said. The door sealed behind him with a quiet *clunk*.

Evie stared at the closed door. "I'm not sure if this is real or not. Maybe it's just a dream, or more likely a nightmare. I'll wake up in a moment and scream in horror, I'm sure."

"Neither, Evie. I promise. Please believe me, even if you don't yet trust us, or me, fully."

"You keep asking me to believe in you and to trust you." She stared at Hesta. "I'm trying, all right?"

"All right," Hesta said. "I just needed you to know how much I want to put this right."

"So you say."

"Shall we go into the library first, then?"

"Even though I can't read?"

"Oh, this goes beyond reading, Evie, way beyond."

"I don't know…"

Hesta held out her hand. "Take my hand, Evie. Let me show you what we are doing."

Take my hand, Evie thought. Only one person had ever said that to her. Was that a sign to trust, at least for the moment?

She reached out, and Hesta's fingers entwined with hers.

"This way," Hesta said, and smiled. "You won't regret any of this, I promise."

6

Evie had never seen so many books. The room was so large you could fit a small house into this one room. Apart from two doors and a small window, every wall was covered with floor-to-ceiling bookshelves, and all of them were filled with books.

In the middle of the room sat a large desk with a chair. Papers and books littered the top.

To one side, situated under the window, stood a small table accompanied by a battered leather armchair. A stack of books lay in a careless pile on the top of the table.

"Goodness. This is impressive," Evie said. "Agatha would call this a real treasure."

"Very true," Hesta agreed.

"What do you need so many books for?" Evie asked.

"This is all for the task we have in mind. As I said, I've been looking into this for a while."

By the number of books they had, Hesta had to be telling the truth. No one had this many books and this much shelf space on the off-chance they would be filled.

"Come this way," Hesta said, and gestured to the door on the opposite side of the room. The door led to another room.

There were shelves here, too, and most of them had been filled with books. One wall, however, contained a set of glass doors. They were covered with blinds fashioned of thin wooden slats and led to a brick-and-glass conservatory. "We read in here, or discuss what we have read."

"It's impressive, very impressive." Yet as she spoke, Evie couldn't see what they wanted her to see in all of this. She heard the sound of teacups being rattled in the library.

"I think Godwyn has the tea ready. Shall we go and have a cup?" Hesta didn't wait for her reply.

Evie shook her head, but followed on in spite of how surreal the entire situation felt.

"Evie," Godwyn addressed her, "would you like milk with your tea? It's just an ordinary brew, I'm afraid. Hesta has not yet stocked the kitchens with suitable options."

Evie opened her mouth to ask who had stolen Godwyn's mind and stopped herself just in time, "Yes, thank you."

"Did you show her?" he asked. He seemed quite excited by whatever it was that she was to see.

"Not yet. I wanted her to see the rooms first."

He nodded at that. Then he placed Evie's tea and a plate full of biscuits on the small table near the window. "Sit." He gestured towards the comfy seat, and, unsure of herself in this situation, Evie sat.

"Godwyn, get us another chair. One from next door will be fine," Hesta said. She stood at the table and added milk and sugar to her tea.

"Is he all right?" Evie asked.

"Yes, why do you ask?"

Evie smiled ruefully. "He's not the Bethwood I know."

Godwyn came back into the room as she made her observation. He placed the chair near Evie and the window, and then he retreated to the desk. He stared at Evie for a moment. "This is true. I'm not the person I was. Things have changed, and we've moved on."

"You've moved on," Evie half whispered. "You. You have moved on."

"And you should move on with us," he said.

"And where are your thugs, Grobber and Williams?"

"Not here," he answered.

"Godwyn needs different people now," Hesta said.

Godwyn looked at Hesta. "This is true."

"It's a pity you don't read." Hesta stood up and walked to one of the bookcases. She gestured to indicate several of the shelves. "We have so many books because they were sold as part of a house sale and no one wanted these journals."

"Journals? I don't understand."

Hesta picked a slim, leather-bound book at random and opened it up. She read from the first page, "Herein are the journals of Lyba Warton."

"It's like a memoir kind of thing?" Evie asked.

Hesta continued to read, but she chose a place several pages in. "Today, on my tenth birthday, I discovered the Mother's Gift within me. I listened to my own mama and not only did I hear the words that she spoke, I heard words she did not say but which were in her thoughts. Papa's, too." Hesta closed the book.

She looked at Evie once before she selected another leather-bound journal. This time she didn't read the introduction but turned a few pages in. "I remember the first time the flames in the fire moved at my command." She didn't read any more but selected another. "...I was arrested by the constabulary for witchcraft. It was hard to understand why, when I'd just saved his life. There are not many that can control bleeding as I can."

Hesta closed the book and put it back on the shelf.

"They're all accounts from gifted people?" Evie asked.

Hesta nodded. "Some, yes."

Evie didn't know what to say.

Godwyn picked up a book from his desk and opened it to

the first page. "Evie Chester, gifted." He read out. He paused to watch Evie's reaction, but she couldn't say or do anything. He continued, "These are not her words, but the words of those who have observed her gifts."

Evie slumped in her seat.

Godwyn closed the book, though. "I'll not read any more, because there isn't any yet. You know what you can do. Maybe you will be able to add to these journals one day."

"How did you get them?" Evie asked.

"As I said, a sale, but no one could be bothered to read the contents. An associate found them and offered them to us. They thought they were just diaries. Thank the mother they didn't look too hard. "

"I want to learn to read," Evie said. "Now more than ever."

"Then I'll teach you," Hesta said.

Evie rose from her seat and took a closer look at the books. "All of these are about gifted?"

"Yes."

"What about syphons?"

Hesta reached out and touched Evie's arm. "I'm sorry, there is nothing here. At least nothing we've found."

"But there might be?" Evie couldn't keep the hope from her voice.

"I'm searching for a librarian or an archivist of some sort to help go through what we have and create a better way to find information," Godwyn said. "That reminds me." He opened one of the desk drawers and drew out a folder filled with scraps of paper. "There are a couple of other things for us to look at, Hesta."

"The Brotherhood of Vitalists?" Hesta asked.

"Exactly. They're running experiments every night this week, and they even have demonstrations at the university. The Institute of Medicine is very keen to see them, especially as Galeazzi Poul himself is there."

Evie couldn't sit back and not understand what they were talking about. "What is this? And who is Galeazzi Poul?"

"You need to understand the whole of it. The background to our position," Godwyn said.

Evie leaned back in her comfortable seat and crossed her arms over her chest. "Go on."

Godwyn also reclined in his seat, as though to mirror Evie. He kept his hands loose in his lap. "As you know, we, and by we I mean I, have been looking at the gifted for a long while."

"So that you could enslave us and use our skills," Evie said.

He shrugged, unrepentant of his actions. "I needed you, and I needed them, too. Now I can do things a different way."

"Godwyn, try not to be so thoughtless," Hesta said.

"If you say so, dear. Anyway. In our look at the gifted, it soon became apparent that there were those who claimed to be gifted but weren't. They deceived people. Then there were those who used deception to abuse their skill not just for their own benefit but to the detriment of others."

"Godwyn started to look at those claims of gift misuse, and together we made a number of observations," Hesta said.

"Most of the deceptions are minor, but people suffer and that will always make ordinary people distrust the gifted," Godwyn said.

"And then they lock us up," Evie said.

"What if we were to change that," Hesta said. She sounded so hopeful that Evie found herself feeling hopeful, too.

"It's just that pretty much every time the normals mix with the gifted, there are too many aggravated incidents. Each time that happens, it's the gifted who are reviled and locked up. I'd rather keep it quiet," Evie said.

"I can understand that. But keeping things quiet doesn't always work out for the best. Does it, Godwyn?"

"It certainly doesn't help," he answered.

"I'm missing something here," Evie said.

"What she means is that Hesta never quite explained her gift to me. She has the most divine singing voice, and people fall in love with her singing. I thought that was it. But it turns out her gift is far more than just the ability to sing well."

"Sometimes keeping secrets is not a good thing," Hesta said.

"We didn't know everything then. And I've had a long time to think about this," Godwyn said. He rose to his feet and paced the end of the room. "I know you think little of me, Evie Chester, but I have good reasons for what I did."

Evie smirked to herself; this sounded more like the Godwyn she knew. "I know."

"It's not just for you, but if I can change the way things are, then I make it safe, or safer, for my sister."

"And make yourself powerful."

Godwyn grunted assent. "There is no harm in protecting your family and trying to get on in the world."

"At my expense. And the expense of others."

"You and the firestarter were probably the last ones."

"Oh!" Evie couldn't keep the surprise from her voice. But that surprise didn't last long. "Forgive me if I have difficulty believing that."

"I understand," Hesta said.

"If you are not going to use the gifted, what were you going to do instead?" Evie asked.

"Doesn't matter anymore. We are on a different path. Except Hesta now insists we should offer some reparations to you and the others. We can do that by creating an institute or an academy. The name is undecided at—"

"I have a tentative name. It's on the papers I gave Evie, but we can change any of the details whenever she likes."

"Right." Godwyn took a moment to get back to what he was about to say. "Anyway, if I can show that gifted people are a benefit to the city, and that these gifted people have the best interests of the city at heart, then maybe we can make a place for the gifted to work."

"What's in it for you?" Evie asked.

"One way or another, it will assist my campaign into political power. That is reason enough. But the most important reason is Hesta. If I can make sure that no one does to her what I did to you, then I would be more than happy."

"That's admirable, but what does that mean for me?"

Godwyn glanced towards Hesta. "You best explain."

Hesta nodded as she began to speak. "In this organisation, you would be an equal partner, and we would look at whatever we thought seemed important. Fraudulent use of gifts, or claims of gifts, and the abuse of the gifted." She stared into Evie's eyes. "You would be paid a retainer of two hundred pounds per annum in the first instance, subject to an increase of one percent per annum."

Evie's mouth dropped open. "How much?" Her voice came out as a squeak.

"Not enough?" Hesta asked.

"By her reaction, I think it might be considered satisfactory," Godwyn said.

"I think I need to think about this some more," Evie said. "And I must take some advice."

"Very wise," Hesta replied. "Godwyn, the letters?"

"Letters?" he asked, then started. "Yes, of course. They are in the desk." He opened another drawer and pulled out a large envelope. He placed it on the table at Evie's side.

"You already gave me papers," Evie said.

Hesta stood at the table next to her. "The papers I gave you were about the whole process. These papers would make it all official."

"I suggest you get yourself serious representation so that you know, for sure, that this is all legal and fair," Godwyn said.

"I wouldn't let it be anything other than fair," Hesta

added.

Evie rose to her feet and turned her back to the room. She looked outside, along the arcaded walkway at the rear of the house into a large walled garden. "I still need to think."

"Why not start straight away with a test case, just so you can experience what we have in mind?"

Evie continued to stare outside, taking a moment before she spoke. "Very well."

"There is a man in town—in fact there are several, but there is one who concerns us most of all. He's been the guest of several people of power and influence, but his motives are unclear."

"Is this the Poul fellow you mentioned earlier?" Evie asked. "Who is he, and what does he do?"

"Exactly him," Godwyn said. "He calls himself a vitalist or a mesmerist, and he makes great claims about the nature of medicine. There are a couple of such people who associate as a brotherhood. From what I can gather, though, he's the main one."

"More than this, he claims he can cure people with the strength of his mind and make it so they do not feel pain during surgery," Hesta added.

"No pain? Is that real?" Evie asked.

"So they claim," Godwyn said.

"But you don't think so?" Evie asked.

"Either they are gifted or they are charlatans. I can't see how it works otherwise," he said. "But they call themselves a brotherhood in Bristelle. They say they have gifts of the Father through the application of the sciences. I don't trust them."

"Are they a religious order?" Evie asked.

"A money-grubbing brotherhood of nothing," Hesta said with feeling.

"Then we better have a look at them, hadn't we?" she said.

7

_____

Evie sat between Godwyn and Hesta as their carriage rattled through the dull and dreary heart of Cainstown district. The houses here were run down and ramshackle. A single, two up and two down, terraced house often provided a home to four families, one to each room. The people of the district called themselves Cainers, and no matter how poor, this was a name of pride to them.

On the edge of the district, there were signs of improvement. Here, the Cainers might live in the small modern houses, which were one room deep and stood back-to-back with an identical house.

People were crammed into whatever they could afford. Sometimes even the free must lead lives that seem little better than the life of a slave.

The carriage took them along the roadway next to the river, with Stake Island always at their side. Evie could barely suppress a shudder. She had been inside one of the prisons on Stake Island. Not as an inmate, but as a way to use her skill to diminish the lives of the poor souls within.

"Are you all right?" Hesta asked.

The question pulled Evie from her thoughts. "Excuse me?"

"You don't look too good," Hesta said.

"Bad memories," Evie answered.

"Of Cainstown?"

Evie pointed out of the window to Stake Island. "That place there."

Hesta turned her attention to the view outside. The dark grey sullenness of the prisons dominated the view. "It's not very pleasant, I agree. But hard to miss from anywhere close to the river."

"No, Hesta," Godwyn broke into the conversation. "Evie has been inside and knows full well the misery that exists within those walls. Don't you, dear?" He almost hid the smirk, but not quite.

"Oh, you poor love," Hesta said, and she reached for Evie's hand.

With the memories of all that she had done within the walls of the prison, the touch of a decent person like Hesta helped to overcome the dark memories. "I did bad things in there, didn't I, Godwyn?"

He sniffed. "You did what you were asked to do. It was necessary."

"Not asked, Godwyn. I was forced. My choices were limited."

"True enough. That was then. And you learned a great deal under my guidance."

Evie stared. She couldn't believe what he'd just said.

"No matter. Your choices are all yours now." He nodded to himself. "Yes, all yours."

Hesta squeezed Evie's hand. Evie looked down at their intertwined fingers and only then realised that neither of them wore gloves. They were skin to skin and nothing untoward happened. In spite of her bad memories, the thought that she could touch someone without ill effect filled her with hope.

She did not let go of Hesta's hand. It was nice, and she took a measure of comfort from the contact.

"Anyway, I'll not allow anything nasty to happen to you," Hesta said. "Although you do know that this is not the finest place to visit?"

Evie snorted. "It's Cainstown. Expectations here are low to non-existent."

"Cynic," Hesta said, but she squeezed Evie's hand again and smiled as she did so. "But you're right. That's why Godwyn is with us. This is not a good place to be without an escort."

They stopped outside a building blackened by the grime of the city and the soot of the nearby dockland furnaces. Godwyn opened the door to the carriage and stepped out. He offered his arm to Evie, and after a brief pause to decide whether to accept, Evie grabbed his arm and stepped down to the ground. She didn't wait for Hesta; she was in a new area and uncertain of everyone and everything.

There were lots of people on the streets. Groups of men, the sort that made Grobber, one of Godwyn Bethwood's enforcer types, look like a posh gent. These men walked where they wanted, without a care for anyone. Poverty of the streets gave a freedom from social mores that Evie had not seen in Ardmore. The women were loud, with little modesty. And as these people rushed by, they left behind a cloud of sweet and sickly perfume, smoke, the odors of the day, and gin. It was not good on the nose.

As the Cainers pushed by without care for the other people in their way, Evie felt her skill flare to life. Many of them would not live long enough to grow grey hair or the wrinkles of old age. Living in Cainstown did not bode well for any of them.

"Come on, don't dawdle," Godwyn urged. He pulled his

timepiece from his waistcoat pocket. "They tend to run these things to a schedule."

Evie looked at Hesta, who slipped her arm through Evie's. "He does like to be punctual these days. Apparently, City Hall demands it."

"Shush, that is not a subject for here," he said. "Come, this way."

There were four men at the door. Grobber types, but that didn't slow Godwyn down. "Bethwood," he said, as though the name meant something. "We're expected."

One of the men shrugged and moved out of the way. "Pay inside."

"Pay?" Evie asked.

Hesta patted her arm. "Yes, they are making money out of this, but Godwyn will sort it out. Let's go in."

As without, so within, and the entrance foyer looked as drab and dirty as the outside. The kind of place where hundreds of people walked through and not one cared about whether the floor had been swept or not. By the looks of it, neither brush nor mop had touched these tiles in a good few years. Black scuff marks from work boots not only marred the floor but seemed to have migrated over the pale green walls. A woman in a plain dress sat at a table in the middle of the foyer. Two Grobber types stood either side and looked menacing.

"Bethwood," Godwyn said.

The woman looked at a small sheet of paper in front of her.

"Preparations have been agreed," he said.

She didn't speak, but nodded when she found his name on the list.

One of the Grobbers pointed down a corridor. "First door on the left, go up the stairs. Seat inside." Then he looked away.

"What do you think, Evie?" Hesta asked as they walked to the indicated door.

Evie pursed her lips. "I'm not sure I should do much thinking here."

"Don't be rude," Godwyn admonished. "You will answer any question when my sister asks."

"No, Godwyn, there's no–" Hesta started.

"It's all right," Evie interrupted. She patted Hesta's hand on her arm to let her know that she didn't hold Godwyn's bad manners against her. "What I think is that half the people we have seen so far are either in the first parts of some sickness, or else they are rather more sick than you think. One of the Grobbers at the door probably won't last the year."

Godwyn's face reddened. The muscles in his jaw tightened and bunched together.

"You did tell her to answer you," Hesta said.

"Some things should not be mentioned aloud," he said through teeth gritted together. "You don't need to call that kind of attention to yourself. Not here."

"And that also gives us the reason why this brotherhood would focus on an area such as this," Hesta said. She stopped walking. "But what's a Grobber?"

"Mr Grobber is one of your brother's enforcers, and they have this way of conducting themselves that seems common amongst them all, no matter what they are called. To me they will always be Grobbers, or hired thugs," Evie said. She smiled sweetly. "Shall we go in now and see how many more walking dead are inside?"

8

Inside the room was pretty full, and they were some of the last to find space. Aside from a couple of tables, it was standing room only. Like any public house in all of the Angles, pipe smoke filled every corner of the dimly lit room. The smell of beer and stale food pervaded every breath Evie took. Here, because most of the audience were men, the sweetness of cheap perfumes did not cover the smells of a working day, and she tried not to breathe too deeply. She'd smelled worse, of course. Anyone who'd lived in an old stable and been left to rot there for days on end knew what smells could be like.

A Grobber type stood next to one of the tables, the only empty one, and they made their way towards him.

"This must be our place," Godwyn said to the chap. "Seating for Bethwood."

The man didn't respond beyond a grunt, but he didn't argue, so he must have agreed. He turned his back and squeezed his way through the crowd at the back of the room.

"I see courtesy is alive and well and not living in Cainstown," Evie said as they sat down.

"For fuck's sake, Evie, just keep your mouth shut and pay attention."

"Language please, Godwyn," Hesta said.

Godwyn turned his attention to the central area, and Evie did, too. There were two chairs and a contraption that looked like a half barrel with iron bars sticking out the side. Two Grobbers brought storm lanterns on tall lamp stands and placed them around the chairs. Their delicate yellow light added to the subtle glow from the gaslight around the walls and illuminated the center well enough to draw attention to one place.

Evie leaned towards Hesta. "Keep your purse close, and don't let go of any valuables you might have."

"Why?" she whispered back.

Evie waved her fingers in front of Hesta's face.

Before she could answer, Godwyn grabbed Evie's arm to get her attention. He nodded. "Agreed." He didn't need to specify exactly what it was that he agreed with, but he released his grip on her arm and looked towards the lit area.

A man in a worn suit walked into the center and guided a young woman to sit in one of the chairs. He appeared reasonably well dressed and clean. He glanced around the room but didn't speak.

The young woman didn't look particularly aware of her surroundings, wore a simple gown, and had bare feet. This would not be the sort of dress to wear out in public, and Evie immediately felt her distrust of this place rise.

Another joined them, a man, escorted by two heavy-set Grobber types. This man looked like one of the homeless men taken off the street. Dirty and unkempt, his ripped and worn clothing barely kept him decent. The man snarled and hissed every step of the way through the room and when they tied him to the other chair. He struggled, albeit weakly, and without making any difficulty for the Grobbers. The man didn't look up, though, and Evie's attention really wasn't on him.

The noise in the room dropped. Attention turned to the performance area, and even Evie found herself staring at the two people in the chairs and the man beside them.

He stopped in the middle of the room and turned in a circle as though to look at all those gathered. "Good evening, one and all. Thank you for attending this rather special event. Today, we have two subjects available for you to see the benefits of the vitalist approach."

He had a quiet voice, carefully modulated, with an accent that didn't belong to Bristelle or the Isle of Mid-Angle. That in itself meant little. As a port and shipbuilding area, there were people from all around the world living in the city. Evie herself had a distinct accent, but this was different again and she couldn't place it. He had dark hair, with grey at the temples. He had brown eyes so dark they almost looked black —a deep, penetrating black.

"Let me introduce you to our guests." He moved to the chair where the girl sat and placed his hands on her shoulders. "This is Alice. Fatherless, born to an alcoholic mother who succumbed to practices we do not mention in decent circles such as this. And so Alice has had a very bad start in life. Her early years were spent in Northside Poor House, and there will be those amongst us who might understand the trials that a young child would experience there."

Evie had to stifle a snort of disdain. But there were several sounds, grunts and sighs from people in the crowd. Many of the Cainers would have had some experience with the poor house.

He touched the girl's shoulder. "Alice, sleep."

He'd barely uttered the words when her head slumped forward. She didn't slip or fall from the chair, though.

"I am Galeazzi Poul, and I've been a Mesmerist, or a

proponent of the Vitalist Movement, for some years. It is the nature of the Mother that makes the tides flow, and yet we know from the science of the Father that the tide's rhythm is because of the sun and the moon. Not faith. Not the whim of a divine force. Science. And so the tides, created by the Mother, affect all things on the earth." He stopped to cast his gaze around the room. Or at least he appeared to do that.

"If the sun and the moon can affect the sea, can it not also affect the body?" he asked.

"That's just daft," a voice called out from the darkness.

"Is it?" Galeazzi answered. "The greatest minds at the university say that man is made up of a great proportion of water. And that the same forces that create the tides of the earth must therefore create tides in the body."

"Astrology. Witchcraft," cried out another voice.

Galeazzi held up a hand. "Science. Always science. Good health is about good tides in the whole of the body." He gestured along his own lean frame. "And when there is a blockage, it causes all manner of problems. Sickness, disease, and more." He tapped the side of his head. "All problems begin and start with the mind. Cleanse the mind and you can cleanse the bodily tides so that health returns, even to a damaged mind." He didn't wait for a response from the audience. "Alice, raise your right hand and hold it before you."

She did as he asked.

He tapped Alice once on the shoulder. "Now then, Alice, when I tell you to, I want you to hold your arm as stiff as a board. No matter what happens, you will not bend your arm. Do you understand?"

"I understand," she replied.

"Good. Now make it stiff."

It was hard to see what happened. But Alice seemed to stiffen all over, as though she were using her whole body to make sure she did as bid.

Galeazzi pointed at one of the men near the front. "Come forward—yes, you sir, please come forward and test Alice's arm."

The man stepped forward. He was a large man, his shirt sleeves rolled up to the elbow to reveal muscular forearms covered with tattoos. He grinned at his friends as if to say it was easy. Alice was a slight young thing. He looked at her outstretched arm as though he expected some trickery.

"What's holding her arm up?" he asked.

"Nothing but her will and the strength of her own arm," Galeazzi answered. "Test her. There will be a limit to the strength on one young woman, so please be reasonable."

The man shrugged and tried to push her hand down. She resisted. He grabbed her hand more fully and used his weight to push down. Her arm faltered a little but held firm.

"Look at her face," Galeazzi said to the crowd., "She isn't even trying, but no matter how much force this man applies to her hand, her arm remains unbent."

The chap tried a different tactic and concentrated on her elbow. But she didn't bend no matter what he did, and now he was getting more forceful.

"Thank you, sir," Galeazzi said. He waited for the fellow to stand away from Alice. "Now one thing, sir, would you be able to hold out your arm this long without showing signs of distress?"

"Of course, I would. What a girl can do, I can do twice as long."

"Would you care to make a wager and test your stamina against hers?"

The man considered her for a moment. "I think I—"

"Thank you," Galeazzi interrupted. "Maybe later. For now, I thank you once more for taking part. Please return to your place." He touched Alice on the shoulder. "You can relax now."

Alice's arm dropped to her lap. She took the instruction literally.

From inside his pocket, he took out a small pouch and removed a substantial needle. "Now, folks, I have spent many hours working with Alice, and not anyone can do these things. I have one more thing to show you." He made sure the whole audience could see the needle as it glinted in the lamplight. "Alice will feel nothing," he said, and he jabbed her with the needle. Blood welled from the stab site, and although Alice didn't respond, Evie flinched and stood up.

Godwyn grabbed her hand. "Sit," he hissed. Evie looked at Hesta, but she sat on the edge of her seat and stared at Galeazzi. Even in the darkness, she looked distressed.

"Hesta," she said to attract her attention. When she didn't respond, Evie sat down and took hold of Hesta's hand. She squeezed very gently until Hesta turned away from the spectacle in front of them.

Hesta stared into Evie's eyes. "I feel something," she said, and touched her temples. "Right here."

"Something gifted?"

Hesta nodded. "I think so." Then she grabbed Evie's shoulders with both hands and pulled her closer. "I think it is someone like me."

"Are you sure?"

"No," Hesta admitted. "But it feels right for someone like me."

Evie looked around at the faces nearby; they all looked at the girl and Galeazzi. Whilst she searched, he continued to stab Alice's arm until drips of blood rolled down to the floor.

"I think you see my meaning?" He pulled a small cloth from his pocket and wiped Alice's arm. "One. Two. Three." He snapped his fingers. "Wake up, Alice."

The girl opened her eyes and looked at Galeazzi.

"I want to show people how easy it is. I'm going to stick the needle in your arm and you will feel nothing."

She shrugged as he stabbed her with a needle. But this time he left it there, stuck in her skin.

"Do you feel anything?" he asked,

"No," she replied.

"Does the needle hurt?"

"No."

"Good girl, Alice. Now you should go into the back room and have a sit-down. I will come to you later."

9

Galeazzi took Alice's seat. "I suppose now would be the time to explain what this is all about." He paused for a moment, and not a single person moved. "It is the tides of the body that control all things, but there is one other force that pervades all animals. We call this force animal magnetism."

He jumped to his feet, and Evie wasn't the only one who reacted to the sudden movement.

"A vitalist is one who understands this force, and like you have seen with Alice, I'm able to take control of these vitals even to the point where she feels no pain." He walked to the fellow who was tied to the chair. "This is Eric."

Eric struggled against the ties for a moment now that attention had moved to him, but he had been well restrained.

Evie stiffened in her chair.

"Eric has an infection of the lungs and the pain is killing him. In fact, he was cured and then re-infected almost immediately."

Now it was Hesta's turn to touch Evie's hand. "Evie?"

"Godwyn, is that him?" Evie asked, her voice low and urgent.

"No," he answered. "Too old."

Galeazzi pulled the spare chair in front of Eric. "Now, I will show you how a vitalist can control the flow of force in another person." He sat so that their knees touched. He straightened his back and placed one hand on Eric's forehead and the other on his chest.

"Look into my eyes, Eric. Let me help you."

Eric spluttered and hissed, but he looked up. For a few moments, it seemed as though they stared at each other in a battle of wills. Then Eric screamed. Galeazzi neither moved nor responded, the cry expected, perhaps.

Evie stared at the two. Her gift didn't seem to work, though; she could see no infection at all. It was as though she'd been locked out.

After another couple of moments, Eric burst into tears. Again, Galeazzi didn't stop. He remained in position until Eric said. "Please stop, it burns."

"One moment," Galeazzi said. "One more moment."

Eric sighed and slumped in his seat. He no longer fought against his bonds, and two Grobbers came into the lit area and released him

"Stand up and tell me how you feel," Galeazzi said.

Eric stood up and took a deep breath. "I feel great, but my name isn't Eric."

Evie's sharp intake of breath drew attention from all around.

"What's up?" Hesta asked.

"There's a mind reader here," Evie said. "Be careful of your thoughts and watch carefully." She looked over her shoulders to see if anyone looked suspicious, but the lighting was too low.

Galeazzi laughed. "The power of the mesmer is so great he is confused." He tapped Eric's shoulder and chuckled away merrily. "Eric, maybe you need a drink after that."

"You are so right, I do," Eric said.

"Good lad." He smiled. "Now that we have seen the

wonders of individual mesmerism, we have spent years creating a way to help lots of people at once." Now he stood next to the half barrel contraption. "We call this the *buquette*. Like a bucket only foreign." He laughed at his own joke and so did the audience.

"Every three days I can recharge the buquette with my own strength and store it for nights such as this. If you have any ill, you can join me in a healing circle. Two shillings a go. Some see instant benefits, and some, those with deep-seated blockages, might need more than one. Either way, the benefits will begin immediately. Come forward. I can only control so much animal force at one time, so don't be slow."

"Two schillings? For some that's half a week's wages," Evie said. Even so, men surged forward in a rush to be seen. They almost threw their coins at him to be included in the magic of the mesmer.

Galeazzi directed them to the barrel. "Grab one of the rods. It is loosely attached so you can guide it to the area of your body that suffers the greatest. With your other hand, touch the person next to you so we make one giant circuit and the force will travel through each one of you." A Grobber type came forward and loosely connected each of them with a thick rope. "The rope has been treated to pass the tide of animal magnetism through you. And the force of the mesmer will be with you."

One of the men looked up in surprise. "I can feel a goodly warmth in my stomach."

Galeazzi clapped his hands. "And so the healing begins."

Before anyone knew it, a queue of willing participants started to form along one side of the room.

"We have to leave now," Hesta said.

Godwyn looked at Hesta and he rushed to her side. "Yes, we will go."

Evie grabbed Hesta's other arm, and they pushed their way through the crowd to the exit.

Godwyn raised his hand to call for his carriage.

"Are you all right?" Evie asked.

"There's someone inside there. Like me. Or not like me," she said.

"A siren? There's a siren in there?" Godwyn asked.

"Something like it, and it completely killed my skills."

Evie thought back to the moment she had tried to look at the sickness in the one called Eric. "I think my skills were also compromised."

"Let's get you both home, and we'll see what we can work out," Godwyn said.

Evie stiffened. "I'm not sure I'm comfortable in your house."

"Not his. Mine," Hesta said. "You were fine there earlier."

Evie relaxed. "That would be fine, then. But it's late, I should go home to think about these things."

10

————

A small two-wheeled calash carriage, the soft collapsible roof folded back, stopped outside the house. Evie watched as Hesta stepped out and came to the door. Even though she expected the knock at the door, and she knew who knocked, still, it made her flinch, and she wondered if that would ever stop. She opened the door nonetheless, and Hesta stood on the front step. She'd chosen to dress simply, plainly, with few signs of her wealth on display, and the obligatory scarf around her neck. That was interesting, Evie thought. She looked at her own clothing. Now they were not so different.

"Hello, Evie."

"Hello, Hesta."

"It's nice to see you."

"I was thinking about you just this morning," Evie said.

"You were? I hope they were good thoughts."

"That depends. I wondered about your throat. I didn't cure it properly, I suppose, and now that you're here, I have an opportunity to try and improve the skin a little more. If you'd like to come inside, I'll try to make your throat a little better. If I do this a bit at a time then I should also get a chance to see what effect I have. If I knew more, then I could do more, I'm sure."

Hesta actually turned an indelicate shade of pink. "Well. Err, yes. I wanted to speak with you about that. It certainly has an effect."

Evie took a step back. "Then come inside. I can take a closer look and try again."

If anything, Hesta took a step backwards. "Later. As I said, I'd like to talk to you about it first."

"Oh? Did I do something wrong?"

Hesta shook her head vigorously. "No, no. Not at all. We just need to talk about how to approach the problem."

"Sure."

"But later. Right now, I have plans." Hesta grinned, and then bowed with a great flourish of her hands. "Your carriage awaits, my lady."

"Get on with you," Evie said.

She tried to hide the heat in her cheeks as she closed the door behind her, but she wasn't sure Hesta hadn't noticed. She grinned too much. "I think you're making fun of me," Evie said.

The driver turned to her and raised his cap. "Good day, ma'am."

"Good day to you, Charlie," Evie said.

Hesta helped her into the carriage and closed the short half height doors. "Never. Furthest thing from my mind. I would very much like you to enjoy the day and the demonstration later, but as to making fun of you? No." She shook her head to underpin her words and her face became serious.

Evie didn't much like the fact that her words had taken the smile from Hesta's face. "I'm sorry. I'm always reminded of our differences."

As they settled inside the carriage, Hesta wrapped a thick woollen throw over their knees. "No, I'm sorry," she said. She leaned back in the seat as she finished wrapping them in the blanket. "I should be more considerate. You've had a difficult time, I know. I just wanted to undo the hardship you've endured, at least a little, and show you that there are better options." She banged on the side of the carriage door. "Onwards, driver."

As though she spoke directly to the horse, the carriage rocked on its wheels and they moved forward.

"I hope you don't mind, but I thought we would avoid any of the ferries and go by road," Hesta said.

"I don't mind," Evie replied. Although that meant they would have to go through two districts and cross over at the Toll Bridge.

"I thought that we could stop off at Jacobs Tea House first," Hesta said, then she looked away, "but I'm not sure that's a good idea."

"No, probably not." Evie stared straight ahead at the back of the driver and thought of her words. "But maybe there is someplace else we could go, more in keeping with my station in life."

"Really, you would?"

Evie turned her attention to Hesta. "Yes. I enjoy your company, but I don't like when our differences are made more obvious. You really don't need to put so much effort into trying to impress me. I have no interest in wealth or status." She snorted. "I have neither."

"I'd be honoured to take you wherever you felt comfortable." She leaned forward in her seat. "Charlie, I think we should go to the tea house at the rear of the old shipbuilders' yard. The one just before the town council and municipal archives."

"The one on Elluth Street?" the driver asked.

"That's the one," Hesta replied.

"I hope it's not posh," Evie said.

Hesta chuckled. "No, it's where the shipbuilders used to

eat, and it's where the poorer students go, along with the people who work at the municipal buildings."

"Right."

Hesta bit her fingernail. "I hope you like it there."

Evie, taken with the effort to make her feel comfortable, sat back in her seat as the coach moved forward. "I'm sure I will. Then we can talk about this mesmerist. And about your neck as well."

"Of course, yes," Hesta said. She stared out the side of the coach and neither spoke for a while. The carriage clattered through the streets of Ardmore, and the noise as they drove through the rough streets of Cainstown rendered conversation impossible.

"Are we going to the house?" Evie asked over the din.

Hesta shook her head.

They didn't turn off where she expected either, nor did they cross the bridges there. Instead, they continued around and crossed the river nearer to the Toll House to the northwest of the city.

She could see the trees and greenery of Queens Park and Castle Hill. The remains of the old fortified manor remained at the top. They drove past the Crescent, a terrace of posh houses that faced the park. Elluth Street stretched behind the Crescent, and Charlie pulled up outside a small, nondescript terrace. A small wooden sign next to one of the doors showed a cup and saucer in the universal symbol of a tea house.

Hesta alighted from the carriage first and offered her hand to Evie.

Evie stared at the offered hand and grinned as she accepted it. No gloves again. They were skin to skin, and Evie thought it was nice to touch someone without something nasty happening. It felt nice, anyway.

"And if it is the sort of place that I can afford, I'll pay," Evie said.

"Good. Tea on you, I think." Hesta turned to Charlie. "We'll be here for a while if you need to drive elsewhere."

"It's all right, ma'am. I'll go and settle myself facing the park, if that's all right?"

"Of course it is. Go and get yourself a cup of tea or something first."

"Yes, ma'am."

Hesta pushed the door open and stepped inside the small house. The tearoom had a few small tables and chairs, but it also had one feature that Evie had not seen often, apart from in one of the small inns near the market: a shelf that stretched along one wall. A single man, his cap pulled low, leaned next to it. He held a book in one hand, and his other rested close to a large cup of tea sitting on the shelf. Evie wondered why he didn't take a seat, but that wasn't her problem.

Hesta found them a table and draped her jacket over the chair next to her. "It will get busy later, but for now, we have a little peace."

Evie looked at the other patrons, the chap standing with a book in his hand and a man by the tiny widow reading a broadsheet. They were not finely dressed. There were no fancy paintings or shiny marble *things*. The floor was hardwood, the walls whitewashed and plain. The tables looked used and none of them were the same. It looked just like the places she would go to near the market. A man in an apron stood behind a small waist-high counter.

"What can I get ya?" he called out.

"Hesta?" Evie asked.

"Tea, please, and a slice of fruit cake if you have it."

"We do," he answered.

"Same for me then," Evie said. She sat opposite Hesta. "How much is it here?"

He must have heard her question because he called out again. "Prices on the chalk board."

Evie looked up in dismay at the scribbles. It meant nothing to her.

'A penny each for the tea, and ha'penny each for the cake,' Hesta said inside her thoughts.

Evie would have been annoyed at the intrusion, but by speaking thus, she was saved embarrassment. Not that she cared what anyone thought, but it was nice of Hesta to be thoughtful.

She closed her eyes to concentrate. *'Thank you,'* she replied, and hoped Hesta heard her.

"You're very welcome," Hesta said aloud. "I hope you like the tea and cake here."

"I'm sure I will," Evie replied. She let her gaze travel over the whole of the room. It was neither a big room nor grand. She liked it. "Do you come here often?"

"Yes, I do," she answered. "It's close and very suitable for my income."

Evie's mouth formed a small "o."

"Are you surprised by that?"

Evie nodded.

"I'm not rich."

"But—"

"But I spend Godwyn's money on accounts, like at Jacobs. After all, what are older brothers for, eh? But not too often."

Evie chuckled to herself and lowered her gaze to the top of the table. "An older brother would be nice."

"You can borrow mine any time you like."

Evie laughed out loud. "I don't think so."

"Just a thought."

The man behind the counter bought them their tea and two plates with a good and generous portion of fruit cake on each one.

"Enjoy," he said, and then left them alone. The man with the newspaper gathered his belongings and left at the same time.

"How is your neck?" Evie asked. "Will you let me check it out later?"

"About that." Hesta looked rather discomforted by the question.

"Is something wrong?"

"Actually, that's it, there isn't. Not really." She reached out to grab Evie's hand. "When you do what you do, there are consequences. It affects more than just my neck."

"I don't understand."

Hesta lowered her voice and almost whispered, "Well, when you touch the scars, in the way that you do, it doesn't just affect the skin there." She pointed at her neck so that there could be no confusion. "It extends further. It extends everywhere."

Evie frowned. "But I only touch the problem area."

"This isn't easy to explain, Evie. You do know about the birds and the bees, don't you?"

"Hesta! Of course I do."

"Good." Now she whispered. "When you do that thing," she gestured at her neck again, "I feel it like, well, like a lover's touch."

"A *what*?"

Hesta laughed and spoke into Evie's mind. *'It's a very intimate touch, Evie. Very personal.'* She cast her eyes in an exaggerated slow glance downwards.

Evie sat back. "Ohh!"

"Does it have the same effect on everyone?"

"I... I... I don't know. Never thought to ask," Evie admitted. "I don't think so, though." She wasn't sure.

"If I were to make a suggestion, I'd say that perhaps it would be better, after all, if few people knew exactly what you can do."

"But what can I do, exactly?"

"We need to find out. And I know someone who can help."

"Who."

"Oklah Wehari."

"I've heard of her; they call her the witch, don't they?" Evie asked.

"She is more than that. Much more."

"All right. We'll go to see her, then. But that reminds me, what are we going to do with the mesmerist business?"

"That's another problem. My brother is making more enquiries."

11

_____

E vie sat in the carriage as they drove back to Cainstown. When asked, Charlie had known exactly where to go. They drove through the more built-up areas to the east side back-to-backs, through narrow streets crowded with people who had no place better to go and children who would never make it to any school.

They stopped at the end of a narrow street, surrounded by other houses. Kids squealed and shouted to each other. They played an aggressive and rather physical form of 'kick the can,' which already looked to have resulted in a bloody nose and several scraped knees.

"Here?" Evie asked. Everyone stopped what they were doing to stare at the carriage.

"Yes." Hesta nodded and got out of the coach.

She was so concerned about the area that Evie didn't think twice when she held on to Hesta's hand to get out behind her.

"I'll wait," Charlie said without prompting.

"Thank you." Hesta strode to a plain door with a small quartered circle on it and knocked twice.

After a few minutes, a young girl, no more than six or seven years old with dark brown skin and black hair, opened the door. She was dressed in a simple white dress, but unlike many of the people outside, her dress looked spotless.

"Come," the girl said, and opened the door wide.

Hesta stepped inside and pulled Evie in with her.

The scent of countless herbs assailed Evie's nose as she crossed the threshold. Food smells joined the herbs, and it smelled lovely. Homely and welcoming.

The young girl closed the door behind them and pushed passed them. "Come in, come in. Gramma always waiting."

Like many of the back-to-backs, this was also a one-up, one-down design., but screens had been used to separate the downstairs room into parts. There was not much furniture, but it had a couple of chairs, a table, and a small iron stove that provided winter heat and a place to cook. Most of the walls had been covered with shelving upon which there were bottles and boxes of herbs and miscellany.

Oklah herself, a large and older woman, sat in a comfortable seat at the back of the room, a book open on her lap as she twisted string, herbs, and corn into a complex pattern. Her eyes were the white of the blind, and the brightness contrasted against the dark brown of her skin. Yet she had a book on her lap and regarded the creation in her hands as though she had no issues with her vision.

She wore a pale linen tunic with the edges embroidered in bright and geometric patterns that were not considered a part of Bristelle or even Anglish fashion.

"Sit," Oklah said. "I finish this."

Evie found a small seat, and Hesta took the other. They waited until Oklah put the token she'd made on one side.

"So you need me?" she asked them in an accent that Evie could not place.

"Yes, Mother Wehari. We are in need of your guidance," Hesta said.

Oklah stared at them with sightless eyes, and Evie found it most disconcerting. She wanted to leave.

"You don't need to rush away from me, Evie Chester," Oklah said.

A cold wave of fear washed through Evie and settled like a block of ice in her gut.

"You come to me for help, and help I will give you." The woman smiled. "You don't know me, but I know you, or of you. Do you know who I am?"

"You are Oklah—"

"Don't be making fun of me; that is not what I meant and you know that."

Evie took a deep breath. "I'm sorry. I feel out of my depth here."

The woman nodded and seemed satisfied with her answer. "I am Old Mother Oklah Wehari, and I am a keeper of the old lore, an Old Wife. I carry with me the knowledge of my mother and my grandmother and all the mothers before me. I use this knowledge of our ancestors to make well those around me. I use my skills and my gifts to ease them through this difficult life."

"And in Cainstown, life is very difficult indeed," Evie answered.

"This is very true. But as you can see, I have a very good life here, and I am very cared for, because the people know they need me," Oklah said.

"And they are terrified of you, because they say you are a witch," Evie said.

Oklah laughed, a deep booming sound that made Evie smile. "I like you, Evie Chester, and I'll do all I can to assist."

"Will you consult a book you cannot see to mix herbs and use symbols to tell me who I am?"

"No, child, I will use my gift. I will see what the Mother wills that I see."

"You're gifted?"

Oklah snorted. "Of course I am. How do you think I see books with dead eyes, huh?"

Evie looked away and focused on a pot of herbs on the floor next to Oklah's seat.

"You have come to me because you are a syphon, and such one does not exist, as far as most are concerned. But even if you don't exist, here you are."

Evie narrowed her eyes to look at the woman more closely. "Who are you? What are you?"

"I am an Old Wife. I make tisanes, lotions, and potions in the way of our mothers, to make the people of this world feel better able to face the ills around them. And the people of Cainstown need me more than any other in Bristelle. I will say the same thing over and over every time you ask me that question." She closed her eyes and opened them in an exaggerated slow blink. "But when I see with my blind eyes, I get to see who you are."

"And who am I?"

"A woman who uses her gift to heal people. An honourable woman driven to do things that don't sit well with her heart."

Evie nodded, more to herself.

"I see your soul, Evie Chester, but it is not a soul born of mortal men and women." Oklah held out a pudgy hand with fingers gnarled by age. "Take my hand."

Take my hand, these were such important words. Evie stared at the hand, but she did not reach out. She expected to see her gift rise up at the sight of those swollen fingers, but nothing came to her. If anything, the woman glowed with health and vitality.

"I won't hurt you," Oklah said. "Take my hand."

Hesta reached over and patted Evie's arm. "It's all right."

Evie closed her eyes. Did they know how important the words 'take my hand' were? At least to her.

She reached out and did as Oklah bid.

Oklah's skin felt dry and hot to her touch. Warmth flooded through Evie, as though she'd spent her entire life frozen until this moment. When Evie looked at the old woman's face, it seemed to glow with inner light.

"I don't need you to heal me, Evie Chester," she said, "but I needed to get a feel for you." She let go of Evie's hand.

"And? Did you truthsay me or something?"

"Or something. I can't tell if you are telling the truth at any one time. Nothing like that. But as well as seeing the world with blind eyes, I can *see* into the essence of things."

"Like my soul?" Evie asked.

"The sum of who you are. You have done things you did not want to do, and yet the goodness of your choices overwhelms even the worst that you have done."

"I have killed someone."

"I know. But that was not your choice but a matter of survival, I think."

Evie nodded.

Oklah smiled at Hesta. "I'm parched. The tea on the stove should be ready to drink if you'd be so kind as to pour. Milk and sugar for me."

"Of course," Hesta replied.

Oklah turned her white eyes back to Evie. "So I will keep this simple. You are not a healer; that is merely a wonderful effect of your gift, and you could use it better if you were to study the body."

"Like a nurse?"

Oklah nodded. "Nurse, medic, or just a person who studies well enough. But you know this already. You are a syphon." She pinched her fingers together as though gripping something unseen. "You take something from here and move it somewhere else." To demonstrate she swept her hand to one side and opened her fingers as though to let it go.

"Like I do with sickness," Evie said.

"As you can do with anything that has no place here, or in this world."

"Like a demon?"

"Very much so." Oklah stared at her, but Evie instinctively knew that this was not the time to speak. "What do you know of the void?"

"Nothing."

"The void is the place that lies between each and every one of the realms of creation. They say the void is empty, but it isn't. A void of nothing allows us to feel secure in the worlds in which we live. It is not a reality." She held out her hand so Hesta could give her a cup of tea. She sipped at the steaming brew without any regard for the heat of the liquid.

"That's better," Oklah said. "So the void. A place of great ill will. And somehow, in your distant past, you have been given blood of the void."

"Does that mean I'm not human?" Evie asked.

"Oh, you are very human. It is your parentage, or rather your ancestry, that gives you a touch of the void. Just as she," she waved at Hesta, "has a heritage in hell itself."

Evie turned to Hesta, and she stared at Oklah.

"You never mentioned that before," Hesta said.

"You never asked the right question," Oklah answered. Then she grinned, all teeth and brightness. "Or maybe it is only now that this might be revealed to you. As you are both here, and your futures are forever entwined."

"Oh," Hesta said. "Looks like there is no escape then, Evie."

"As long as you keep your brother under control, she'll have no problems with you," Oklah said.

"I'll do that, then, and I'll make sure she's safe," Hesta said.

"You do know I'm here, right?" Evie said.

"I do know," Oklah answered.

"What about the mesmerist?" Evie asked. "There's something not right about that whole situation."

The seer thought about it for a few moments. "The mesmerist has a certain scientific way about him. Or he did.

The mesmers around the world are having some beneficial impact, but it is too soon to say when these skills are masked by gifts."

"That's what I thought. I couldn't see the sickness they were talking about," Evie said.

"Maybe there was no sickness," Oklah suggested. "Or there was someone reading your minds? Or were they simply interfering with what you saw?"

"Another siren was my thought," Hesta said.

"More like a sonos," Oklah said. "One who has a different ability to yours, Hesta. There are many sonos in the world and they each carry that gift in different ways."

"Do they have any other abilities? Could they hurt people?" Hesta asked.

Oklah shook her head. "I do not know. I cannot see anything about this at the moment. Just be careful. Be very careful indeed."

"We will." Hesta stood up. "Thank you so much for your time and your knowledge."

Oklah inclined her head to one side as though hearing something. "Any time. If you need help again, come back. Maybe I will see more for you." She waved at the table. "There is a small brown package with a sprig of sage through the string. That is for you. You cannot come to the Old Wife without taking away a medicine. Make a tea, for both of you, and drink it hot. No milk and only a touch of honey. It will do you good. That will be thruppence. Leave it on the table."

"Yes, Mother," Hesta said. She picked up the package and left a short stack of two shilling pieces, a rather larger sum than the one requested. "Thank you," she said as they left.

12

_____

The chambers of Packer and Blewitt, Solicitors and Associates at Law, Society of the Angles, were located right at the end of Ardmore Street, in the posher end of Salverton. Evie and Agatha sat in the offices of Alfred Packer, one of the partners of the law firm.

He smiled broadly, and with genuine humour. "Agatha Hickman, it's been far too many years. I never thought to see you again, more's the pity."

"Now here I am again," she said.

"I admit, the moment you made contact, I thought you'd found yourself in a spot of bother."

Agatha chuckled. "If I ever found my way to trouble, then you'd be first to know."

"Good," he said. "But the matter at hand is not one of bother, so that is good."

He opened a brown card folder on his desk and read a series of notes written in black fountain pen.

"So, what do you think?" Agatha asked. "Is there anything that young Evie should worry about?"

He looked at Evie as though he saw her for the first time.

"Well, Miss Chester, I think you've gotten yourself into a good position."

"Have I?" Evie asked.

"Indeed. This contract means that the formation of this institute or association is to be run in combination with Hesta Bethwood. There is nothing that can happen without Miss Chester's agreement. Even the name and the very nature of the organisation must be agreed between you."

"That sounds remarkably foresighted," Agatha said. "And gives Evie here a great deal of control."

Alfred nodded. "I concur. As I read through the whole document, there are a couple of other things that are also quite singular in their care for the wellbeing of Miss Chester."

"Such as?" Evie asked.

"Did you look at the details, Miss Chester?"

"No, I can't read."

He looked at Agatha.

"I did read through it, but I'm not sure I believed my own eyes," Agatha replied.

"Very well. This organisation is to be controlled only and solely by Hesta Bethwood and Evie Chester." He looked up from his notes to stare at Evie. "As a part of this, you will be given fifty percent of the building known as Bethwood House in Salverton. Do you know it?"

"I know it," she said, but her voice was no more than a whisper.

"In addition to the property, a retainer of two hundred Anglish pounds each year, payable in monthly installments, will be paid to you in whatever manner suits you best. Cash or transfer through the finance system of Bristelle."

Evie's mouth dropped open. "I knew I would get paid such a sum, but the reality of it is still a shock to me. More so that it is written here, all legal and certain."

He nodded. "Of course, this is an extremely generous

salary. You will also be given expenses for travel and whatever else you may need, including access to a contingency fund. Your salary will increase each year at a rate to be negotiated between yourself and Miss Bethwood."

"Holy Mother of us all," Agatha said.

"There are two more things. If anything happens to Hesta, then she has named you the beneficiary of all monies and all properties, including Bethwood House. On your death, then all of your holdings in this organisation will pass over to Agatha Hickman, or to whichever beneficiary you name, and no one else may claim ownership over her."

Evie couldn't speak.

"And the other thing?" Agatha asked.

"Yes. For legal purposes, the organisation is to be called the Chester-Bethwood Academy. Its assets are listed so there can be no confusions." He put his pen down. "As long as this institute works without eroding all of its assets, you are well set up for the future."

"They can't take it away?" Evie asked.

He leaned against his desk, hands clasped in front of him. "No. This is as good a contract as any I have seen. There are forms to go to the land registry and the registration of the academy, but that is something I shall do on your behalf. After you sign, only you can dissolve the arrangement and all reparations are to be met by Hesta Bethwood. Godwyn Bethwood guarantees all monies through his company and the Bank of Bristelle. Miss Bethwood has already signed the contract, and it has been witnessed and stamped by Willard and Peak of Esman Street.

Evie turned to Agatha. "What do you think?"

Agatha paused for a moment. "It sounds like a good contract."

Evie looked at Alfred. "You're the legal person, what is your professional advice?"

He remained still. "It is not for me to tell you what you should do, but this contract has no issues that should cause you harm. If you are interested in this venture, then it sounds well considered."

Evie stared at him for a moment, her thoughts in a whir. "I'll sign it, then. Although I can't read or write."

"Doesn't matter," he said. "I will witness and that will be enough. Also Mrs Hickman can witness, and my apprentice will witness her signature."

"Just do that signature we practiced," Agatha said. "It will be fine."

Alfred stood up and opened the office door. "Jeff, come here and witness this, if you please."

A young man, barely old enough to grow hair on his chin, shuffled over to the side of the desk.

Alfred turned the document so that it faced Evie the right way. He put a pen in front of her and pointed, with his finger, where he needed her to sign. "Here, please."

With great care, she made her rather wobbly sign, a wiggly "E" with an equally wobbly "C"-shaped mark.

"And here as well," he said.

She made the same marks all over again.

Agatha, Alfred, and the young man signed against each of her signatures and dated the document. Lastly, Alfred dropped melted wax on two pages and added his sign to the soft red lump.

"There you go, signed. There are two copies here. One, I shall courier to Miss Bethwood, the other is for you. Unless you wish for me to keep this and keep it safe?"

Evie looked at Agatha, who nodded.

"Please. Errm, how should I pay for–"

"The cost for this meeting, the signature, and the safety of the documents, are part of the costs that the Bethwoods are prepared to pay. There is no cause for concern about my fees."

Evie took a deep breath. "Then it is done and my future is set."

"Looks like it," Alfred said. He stood up and offered his hand. "Good luck to you, Miss Chester."

When they were done, Evie stood outside the doors to Packer and Blewitt. The black front door shone almost as much as the brass door knocker.

"Are you all right, Evie?" Agatha asked.

"I have a job. An income. Enough to pay for Florie, too. I'm not sure if I'm awake or dreaming."

"Well, shall we get a cab home? A nice cuppa is in order, I think, and we can talk about everything."

Evie smiled. "You know what, I'd like to go for a walk through the city. It would be nice to stop and look in the shop windows and not be scared of people. I don't need to be scared anymore, do I?"

"Evie, you're a free woman, and a woman of means now. Bethwood will never be able to take advantage of you again. No one is hunting you anymore. Be free. But be careful, yes?"

"I will. I just want to take in the air and enjoy my freedom. Then I'll get a cab when I'm ready."

"Good." Agatha held up a hand as she spied a small calash and driver. "I'll go home and leave you to it."

Evie hugged Agatha in an uncharacteristic display of affection.

Agatha patted her back. "Whatever was that for?"

"Thank you for everything. For taking care of me, and of Florie, and for being there when we needed help."

Agatha pulled away and held her at arm's length. "I couldn't help but want to help the pair of you. You are always welcome in my home."

"Cab, ma'am?" asked the driver as he pulled up in the small calash.

Evie helped her into the cab, and Agatha sat down with a slump. "Top of Ardmore if you will, number 17."

"Near the gin palace?" he asked.

"That's the one," Agatha answered.

Evie stood back on the pavement and watched as the carriage pulled away. She smiled to herself then as she marched down the street without the need to hide herself. She felt free.

13

The shops of Salverton were bright and filled with luxury items. A tailor's shop displayed a single suit, and not likes the ones of the men who worked in the shipyards either. A seamstress shop offered a very fine gown in one window, and in the other, the clothing and accoutrements for maids and other such downstairs staff.

Evie needed new clothing, but this would be a little too much for her, she thought. She would ask Hesta. And when Evie thought of her, a little smile crossed her face. She saw herself in the shop window and, without terror following her, she looked like any other young woman. A maid, perhaps, but not a slave.

She pulled her shoulders back and, as she turned, a wave of dizziness blurred her vision. Her knees almost buckled, but then the dizziness stopped. She took a moment to right herself and get herself together. Had she had something to eat that hadn't agreed with her? She didn't think that was so. What with the visit to sort out the contract and so on, she hadn't eaten much at all. Maybe she was just hungry.

She found a small tea house, but they stared at her as though she had no right to be there.

"Snobs," she muttered under her breath, and headed down a side street towards the river. She wasn't far from the old shipyards; there was bound to be some place that she could afford. If not, she would make her way to Elluth street.

The dizziness lessened until it became no more than a memory. For a moment or two, she wondered if the whole experience could be put down to the pressure and emotional strain of the past weeks. Her thoughts drifted from the fancy shops she passed and instead she focused on the contract she'd just signed. She had a job.

The market area caught her by surprise. It wasn't a large one. A dozen or so barrow boys and women with baskets. She saw fresh fruit, vegetables piled so high she thought they would topple off the stalls. Fresh-caught rabbits hung from a pole, joints of meat covered in hessian to protect them from the flies that hung about for a free meal. A woman sold flowers from two baskets brimming over with colour. Another sold cloth samplers and gave out papers about where to buy the material by the bolt. For a market, the vendors were quiet, not like the ones in Ardmore. But there were fewer here, so they didn't have to be so vocal to compete for customers.

The sight of all the food made Evie's mouth water, and her stomach grumbled at the lack of food. She bought a small wax-covered round of cheese no bigger than her fist and put it into her pocket for later. A stall selling cooked meat caught her attention, and she purchased a small pork pie to eat right then and there. She took a nibble of the pastry hoping it would fend off whatever had ailed her earlier and drifted through the remaining stalls.

A searing pain burned through her eyes and blurred her vision so much she could barely make out any details of the stalls or the surrounding people. She made it to the edge of the market and along the nearest street. There were fewer people here, and the shops were smaller, but still not the sort of establishments in which she felt comfortable.

Another wave of dizziness almost brought her to her knees as she walked along Great Herman Street. A great screeching echoed inside her ears, and the pain in her head grew almost too great to bear. She wiped her eyes and brushed away tears of pain.

She saw Jacobs Tea House, and in spite of the welcome she'd had the last time, she headed there. She opened the door and had barely stepped across the threshold when a waiter came straight to her. The waiter stared at her for a moment and then recognised her. "Well good day to you, Miss Chester. Can I show you to a table?"

She looked at him as though he'd grown two heads. "Arthur," she said. "I'm surprised you recognized me. I have only been once before."

"Yes, of course, but there are not many people vouched for by the Bethwoods. And of course, your coloration is not the most common in Bristelle."

"Of course." For once blonde and blue eyed helped her. "Arthur, I think I need something light to eat and some black tea with milk and honey."

"Of course, of course. You look white as a sheet, if you don't mind me saying."

"I don't feel at my best."

"Perhaps you'd prefer a restorative tea, a delicate pink with herbs and not too spicy?"

"I have no idea what that is."

"Will you trust my judgement, Miss Chester?"

She nodded, but the pain that shot between her eyes made her wish she hadn't.

"Well, let's get you seated, and I'll get the tea straight away."

"Thank you," she managed. Thankful to sit down, she leaned her elbow on the table and rested her head on her fingers. Alfred didn't take long to bring her tea, and along with it, a slice of cake. "Will Miss Bethwood be joining you?"

"No. No one knows I'm here. I just need to recover, and then I'll go home."

"Very well. You should drink the tea while it's hot, and the cake is a very light sponge so as not to aggravate the stomach. Take a bite; it might help settle you."

She sipped at her tea without even noticing the taste. Likewise with the cake. She took a bite, chewed, and swallowed. The pain in her head grew worse, like every engine in the whole of Bristelle had decided to flare up inside her skull. She could barely think. Her thoughts dashed from one thing to another, and she couldn't gather her thoughts in any kind of coherent fashion. And it hurt. As though her thoughts were beating against the inside of her skull.

The world turned grey and nondescript. Even the teacups and the plate with the sponge seemed grey and faded almost to nothing. Her thoughts merged into one thought and the thought was grey.

She came to with a start. Hesta knelt at her side and looked worried. "Evie, will you answer me?"

Answer? Evie could hardly hear the words, never mind understand them.

"Evie."

She looked up, and as she did, Hesta pressed her lips against hers.

She didn't respond. A part of her thought she should have been outraged at the uninvited contact. Another part hardly recognised it at all.

Hands grabbed her and shook her. She didn't fight or resist it, there seemed no point. She let go of her body and slumped back. It seemed easier, somehow; the less effort she put into herself, the less she hurt.

She knew when she'd been slapped across the face. It stung a little, but in the scheme of things it was no more than a gnat bite, and she ignored it. She closed her eyes and let herself sink into the depths of grey.

A single command seared through the murk and blew it away in an urgency that had no place in the softness of the grey. "Kiss me," ordered a soft voice. "Kiss me like you mean it."

Evie ignored the command. It was too little against the surge of the grey.

"Kiss. Me." This time she could hear the echoes of music behind the words. Like a song, and she couldn't stop herself from reaching out to hear more of the melody.

"Come on, Evie, kiss me. Listen to my song and feel my kiss."

Something soft brushed against her lips.

It was nice.

The song grew louder inside her head, and the grey receded a little.

She kissed back, and the pain receded with the drowning depths of grey.

"Kiss me like you mean it," the song insisted. Not with quite the command used before, but insistent and maybe laced with a little humour.

She turned her head slightly to one side, and the lips met hers better. It wasn't just nice, it was very nice. Heat flowed through her body and chased the cold of the grey away. Music swirled and echoed inside her head. She pulled Hesta closer.

The pain, the headache, and the nausea dissipated completely. She found herself staring into Hesta's concern-filled eyes. She could melt into those brown eyes.

Then the kissing stopped. Now her thoughts were her own once more, and Hesta drew back.

"Are you all right now?" Hesta asked. She looked so serious, worried even. "Please talk to me."

"Are you going to kiss me again?"

Hesta laughed. "Only if you want me to."

Evie sat upright, and only then did she realise that Arthur had helped to keep her from slipping over. She looked at Hesta and then at Arthur. "What happened?"

"It seems you had a funny turn, Miss Chester," Arthur said. "I had a runner go and fetch Miss Bethwood straight away."

"Thank you, Arthur. Your timeliness has saved Miss Chester from a great deal of pain. It is appreciated," Hesta said.

"At your service. I think I should make you fresh tea."

"That would be lovely, thank you," Hesta said.

Evie waited for him to walk away before she spoke. "What's going on? I'm sick, and you have to kiss me? That doesn't seem right."

Hesta took Evie's hand in hers and gently rubbed the back of Evie's hand. "No, it isn't right. But necessary."

"I'm not convinced."

"I'm sorry." She stopped as though she had things to say but was holding back. "No matter what else I might say, you were under attack from someone like me, a siren perhaps."

Evie shook her head and was pleased to find that it didn't hurt at all. She still felt a little lightheaded, but not to the extent that she had, and the headache was now no more than a distant memory.

"I don't know. I can't see how the effect you have on people is the same as the drowning ache that I had. It was so painful I could barely think. And then it was like someone was digging through my mind with a shovel and pickaxe."

"That doesn't sound like a siren. It does sounds like a sonos attack, though."

"I know Oklah mentioned such a thing, but it meant little at the time. What's the difference?"

"It's a difference of kind, really. At least, as far as I have gathered so far. We all have different kinds of sonos gifts. The

Siren is just a particular type. Many of the other sonos types are more physical, in a way. A wall of sound can feel like a wall, and if they play with the sound itself then it can have other effects."

"Like?"

"Like the wall, making a noise so painful it hurts the ears. That sort of thing. We know so little about them. So the sonos is something we would need to investigate."

Evie heard the hope in Hesta's voice. "I signed the contract, Hesta, so perhaps now is as good a time as any to start investigating."

"Good."

"Now, about that kiss…"

Hesta looked into her eyes. "I'm sorry. I hope it didn't offend you too much, but a siren's kiss is the only way I could think of to pull you out of that state."

"Hesta?"

"Yes, Evie?"

"It didn't offend me." She looked away, but tried to gauge Hesta's reaction from the corner of her eye. "But next time, it must have nothing to do with gifts or magic."

14

Evie slumped into the carriage that awaited them outside Jacobs. She barely acknowledged Charlie the Driver before closing her eyes and allowing her mind to drift. She imagined putting her thoughts in order, her mind in such disarray it was as though a hard wind had ruffled through the papers of her memories and thoughts. It wasn't pleasant. It was a violation of self.

She shuddered at the idea, and when Hesta grasped her hand, Evie had to fight off the urge to shy away.

"It's all right, Evie. This has not been a good day for you."

Evie opened her eyes so she could look at Hesta. "Thank you."

Hesta squeezed her hand.

"Thank you for making me feel important and giving me a sense of worth."

Hesta appeared momentarily confused. "I've done nothing. I just came to fetch you when Arthur said you were very sick."

"I don't mean that. I mean the Chester-Bethwood Academy."

Hesta turned away as she sat in her seat. "I told you, Evie, you are very important to me."

"Will the sonos come back?" Evie asked.

"I don't know."

"Can you deal with him? Her? Whoever it was?" Evie asked.

"We shall try."

Evie wasn't too keen on the lack of certainty, but there was nothing she could say to change that. "Most importantly, why was I attacked?"

"That is a most interesting question. I'm going to have to involve Godwyn. He has a better mind for this kind of thing."

Evie shrugged and closed her eyes. It wasn't that far to travel, but the roads in Salverton were better, smoother, and less rumbly even than the main road through Ardmore. The next thing she knew, Hesta was shaking her.

"Wakey, wakey, sleepy head," she said with a smile. "Better get you inside."

"Where are we?"

"My house. I can make sure that you're well, and if there is another attack then I want to be there to deal with it."

"Agatha will be expecting me."

"I'll get a runner to send a message, and when you're better, you can go home. Or stay here? We have plenty of space. Anyway, don't worry about the details. Let's get you inside so we can make sure you're all right."

"I'll be fine."

Hesta helped her out of the carriage. "Let me be the judge of that. Let me look after you."

"I can manage."

"Of course you can, but I've not met anyone who has been attacked like you have."

"Well, make me another cup of tea, then, and we'll see if my head explodes whilst I wait."

Hesta snorted and offered her hand. "Come into my lair, and I'll see if I can manage the tea."

This time, Evie didn't even pause before she accepted the offered hand.

They settled in the drawing room. A small stove provided enough heat to chase away the chill of the room. The armchair and a small couch looked comfortable and well used, and an occasional table with a short but decorative lamp stood off to one side. Oak cabinets and shelving gave the room a rather cosy air.

"Let me take your coat, and make yourself at home," Hesta said.

Evie let her coat fall from her arms and realised that there were weights in the pockets. She stuck her hand in one pocket and pulled out the cheese. From the other she pulled out a pork pie with its partly nibbled pastry case.

"Did you have a mouse in your pocket as well?"

"I was hungry!"

"I'll get plates and some bread and pickles to go with this feast. Unless you wanted to save them for Mrs. Hickman?"

"I can get more, but I could do with more to eat."

"Coming up," Hesta said as she left the room.

Evie waited a few moments and then she too left. She headed straight for the library. She still couldn't read, but Agatha had taught her how to identify the letters of the alphabet, and she could already read numbers, too.

Each of the shelves filled with the journals and observations of the gifted had a brass cardholder with words written on it. Although she'd started to identify each of the letters, they meant little as yet. But she did recognise the letters. She focussed her attention so intently on the books and the labels that she didn't hear Hesta enter.

"Anything take your fancy?"

"Not yet," Evie replied. "But I see that they are all arranged alphabetically."

"I thought you couldn't read."

"I can't. Agatha has been trying to teach me letters and numbers."

"If you know the alphabet already, you're making excellent progress."

"No, it's very slow." Evie made her way along the brass labels and stopped when she got to the letter 'S'. "This is 'S,' so this must be where we find sonos, siren, and syphon. Show me what you have."

Hesta pulled out a substantial journal. "This is about sirens, and it's mostly all about me and what I have seen."

"And the sonos?"

Hesta replaced the siren file and drew out a slimmer one. "This is what we know about the sonos gift. There isn't a lot here, because there isn't much known about them."

"And is there one on the syphons?"

Hesta selected another slim journal. A brand new and unused one. She opened it up and the pages were blank. "I need you to help me fill this out. If you want to, that is."

Evie rubbed her temples. She no longer had a headache, but her thoughts were still fuzzy.

"Are you all right? Do you have a headache?" Hesta asked, concern in her voice.

"No, it's no more than a remnant of earlier. It was very unpleasant. What did they do to me that you were able to make the pain go away?"

"As I said, the sonos, in general, uses sound and pressure so it seems as though they have control over the air itself. It also seems to be a very individual skill."

"So each one is different?"

"Kind of. Some say that a siren is a type of sonos, the mermaids, too. But we're a specific type of sonos, if you like."

"You sing."

"Yes. But singing just makes it more pleasant to hear. Sometimes I can use sound, like the sonos."

"Are all sirens the same?"

"Sirens use their gift to confuse and beguile so they can get what they want, I suppose. The other types of sonos are too varied to make a single judgement."

Evie considered that for a moment. "I can accept that. But I still want to know why they would attack me?"

"I have no idea. I think we should speak to Godwyn about it."

"If we must."

"He is good at this kind of thing."

"Maybe now that I am here, I should do something more for your neck," Evie said.

"You need to rest for the moment and not stress yourself."

"All right, but maybe we should sit in the drawing room with our tea. And maybe you could read to me about what you know about sirens and sonos."

"I'd like that," Hesta said.

"If you sat next to me, then you could show me the words, too."

Hesta grinned so broadly that even Evie had to smile back. "I would love to."

"But first, I want to know the truth of why you want to help me so much. And I want the whole truth. I couldn't possibly trust anyone who was not totally honest with me."

"I agree. Let me just get something else before we go." Hesta crossed to a bookcase across the room and ran her fingertip along the spines of the books. "Ahh here it is," she said and slid another journal from the shelf.

"What's that one about?"

"I have a couple of books on the siren. The other is full of conjecture and myth. But this one—this is a very specific book. It's my story. I'd like to read a little of it to you. And when you know my story, you can keep my book until you learn to read it for yourself so you can see that what I say is my truth."

Evie nodded. "All right."

"First, let's make ourselves comfortable in the drawing room. I think I'm going to need a cup of tea."

They sat facing each other on the couch. A pot of tea sat on the table, and Evie poured out two cups. "Tell me your story," Evie said.

Hesta started at the beginning and flipped through the pages slowly, as though to reacquaint herself with her own history. "Godwyn and I were orphans, you know that?"

"Yes, I recall that much."

"Although we are not related by birth, we've become related by hardship."

"I know that as well. You both had so much pain, yet you inflicted more on others."

"I have no excuse. We did what we needed to survive, and in the process, I think we lost a part of ourselves."

Evie nodded.

Hesta stared at the book. "When they came and took my voice, we used every healer we could find. And then I went to see Oklah Wehari."

"I thought you might have been before."

"You're right, I have. I've been a few times over the years."

"What did she say?" Evie asked.

Hesta closed the book and leaned back. She stared at the ceiling for a moment and then closed her eyes. Now it was Evie's turn to seek out Hesta's hand and offer what comfort she could.

"She said there was nothing she could do to help. She said there was nothing I could do to help myself. I was damned, she told me, damned for eternity, and I should accept my fate gracefully."

"I'm sorry."

Hesta opened her eyes, but they were lost now to memories and had no focus. "Later on, she said that I would have one chance of redemption, and if I didn't take it then all would be lost for me. But no matter what I did, I would pay for being born."

"And you've been back to see the woman who said that?"

"Because she was right."

"You're not damned," Evie said.

"She also said I needed to make amends, and I would know what that meant when the time came." The corners of Hesta's mouth quirked, almost to the point of a smile. "I think that time is now. After the last visit, I know I am some sort of a hell spawn thing, and so I think I might be an accursed creature after all."

"We're two strange beasts, one from hell and the other from the void. Let's not worry too much about such minor details, shall we?"

Hesta turned to Evie. "I can sing and charm. For me that has always been the extent of my gift, but then I had little reason or time to discover the full potential of my voice."

"What do you mean?"

"My gift did not present itself until after I changed from a child and into a woman." She smiled ruefully. "It is almost as though I needed to grow breasts before my full siren song could be heard."

"Did you have no idea before then?"

"Not really. I had a good voice and people loved to hear me to sing, but I wasn't a full siren. When my gift blossomed, I had no idea what I could do with it and I had no one really to ask."

"You could have asked your brother," Evie suggested.

Hesta shook her head. "I couldn't. And then no long after that I lost my voice."

"You didn't lose it, your voice was taken."

"Either way, lost or taken I didn't have the opportunity to explore the full extent of my abilities."

"Well, that's something else for us to discover, isn't it?"

"Us?"

Evie patted Hesta's hand. "Of course it is us. Looks like we are tied together. Let's see where it takes us."

15

E vie woke to the sound of a loud bang and froze in place. She'd fallen asleep, but she wasn't in her bed. Long dark hair fell over her face and covered part of her view. A shoulder pressed against her cheek and dampness covered the side of her mouth; she'd drooled.

She sat up once she felt certain that the bang did not represent an immediate threat and tried to stifle a yawn.

"Sleep well?" Hesta asked.

Evie looked around. The shadows from the window were longer now. "Did I sleep long?"

"Not really."

Evie felt heat rise into her cheeks. "I fell asleep on top of you. I'm sorry, that was not very polite of me."

Hesta shook her head. "Nice? It was lovely. To me, it felt as though you trusted me enough to let your guard down. And I'm honoured to—"

"Hesta!" Godwyn bellowed from the hallway. "Where in all the damnations are you?"

"Here in the drawing room," she called back.

Godwyn turned the door handle so hard that the door burst open. "There's an emergency, and Evie is missing."

Only after he stepped into the room did he notice that Hesta wasn't alone. "Oh. Well, that explains why no one can find Evie." He narrowed his eyes. "You two look very cosy."

"Yes, well, Evie came under attack, and I wanted to make sure she was well and safe from any further incidents."

"What? How? When was this?" Godwyn asked. He drew back his shoulders and ground his teeth as though the news was a personal affront to him.

"There is a sonos loose in the city, and Evie was his target."

"For goodness sake, if there has been an attack, you should have informed me."

Evie stood up and faced Godwyn. "You are not my keeper, Godwyn Bethwood."

He glared at Evie. "Yes, I am. Especially now that you're involved with my family."

"I am not your property anymore."

"I am more than aware of the change in the nature of our relationship. Hesta has drawn you to us, and so it is my duty to take care of you, whether you like it or not."

"Do I have a choice?" Evie asked.

"Not really, no," he answered.

Hesta reached for her hand. She did that a lot, and Evie accepted it. She rarely even thought about her fear of touching Hesta anymore.

"Sit with me, Evie," Hesta said. "Then Godwyn can sit down and tell us what the emergency is all about."

He perched on the edge of the armchair, legs apart as he leaned his elbows on his knees. "There is something going on in the city."

"Please elaborate," Hesta said.

He took a deep breath. "It started this morning just after the council meeting, or rather, during the meeting."

"What did?" Hesta prompted him.

Godwyn jerked from his memories. "The headaches came

first. The members of the council had finished discussing my Freedoms for the Gifted Bill. Amendments had been discussed and it all went very well. So well, I thought we'd be given permission to set up the institute. Or at least that the council would allow the Bill to be passed under a probationary agreement."

"And?" Evie asked.

"That's when the chairman grabbed his head and claimed a major headache. Not just him, though. Almost half of the official present were affected. As a result the council ceased and postponed all votes. I thought nothing of it." He rose to his feet and moved next to the fire. "Pockets of sickness have erupted all over the city, but the worst of it is concentrated at the west end of Cainstown and into east Salverton."

"I was in the eastern end of Salverton," Evie said.

"Did you see anyone else who was sick?"

Evie shook her head. "I'm not sure I could think clearly enough to pay attention to others."

"What's going on, Godwyn?" Hesta asked.

He raised his big shoulders and let them slump back down. "I have no idea."

"Godwyn," Evie said, "get Grobber, Wiggins, and your other enforcers together. Get them on the streets. Speak to the street kids and get them to listen to what's going on. If there are any rumours, trouble, strangeness, or anything like that, they'll soon know what they are."

"Those are quite specific instructions," Hesta observed.

"Ask Godwyn. That's how he caught me," Evie said.

"Really?"

"Please, what's done is done," Godwyn said.

"Then do the same to learn something useful. Find out what the people know."

"Very well," he agreed. "But that won't tell us why there are so many sick people about."

"We'll find out the why later, but first, we should help the sick people, especially those in Cainstown."

"We?" Godwyn asked.

"Of course," Evie said. "If there are sick people, then they need help. They do not have access to the medical facilities that some areas do. At the very least, we need to know whether all these events are as related as they seem. What if there is a new epidemic and we're doing nothing about it when we can?"

"Evie's right. We should help," Hesta said. "Do you have your carriage outside?"

"I do," he said.

"Then take us to the heart of the problem, if you know where it is," Evie said.

They rushed through the streets of Salverton in Godwyn's carriage. Evie didn't need to be told when they reached the edges of Cainstown, though. She could feel the pressure building long before they'd reached the slums proper.

"Can you feel it?" she asked.

"Yes," Hesta said.

"Like a storm. A big one," Godwyn said. "The horses don't like it either. I'm not sure I'd want to take them any further." He banged once on the roof of the cabin and opened the door. "Pull over. We'll walk from here."

Evie expected to see more people on the street. Even if they weren't in the heart of Cainstown, the people would still spill into the surrounding areas. The ones here walked along as though they hadn't the strength to stand upright.

"What do you think, Hesta?" Godwyn asked.

"If the sonos was here, I think he's gone."

"What about you, Evie. Can you heal anyone?" he asked.

It took Evie a little while before she could start using her skill and even then it seemed sluggish. "Something here slows down my ability. I have no range at all."

"Is that usual?" Hesta asked.

"No. Nothing interferes with my gift. Well, other than when we went to the mesmer, and then I felt nothing."

"Did you try?" Godwyn asked.

Evie shook her head. "No, but I was aware that I wasn't feeling quite right."

"Are they sick?" he asked.

Evie walked up close to a young man. She avoided the older ones to prevent age from affecting her gift. "Excuse me," she said.

"Stay away," he said.

"Pardon?"

"Don't get any closer. Not if you have brain ache and sickness."

"No, I'm fine. We're healers," Evie said.

"You don't look like no healer."

"Looks can be very deceptive." She looked into him anyway. He was a surprisingly healthy young man. "Where should I head to offer assistance?"

He pointed back down the road. "Head to the river. You'll not miss anything." Then he pulled his jacket closer to his lean frame and slouched off.

"Coming?" Evie asked.

Hesta linked arms with her. "Of course."

Godwyn followed behind. Every few steps he muttered about his head breaking.

Halfway down the street, he stopped, bent over, and held his head in both hands. "I can't go on. Leave me here."

Hesta faced Godwyn. "Stand up straight," she said.

"Please, Hesta, I can't stay here."

He gripped both sides of his head, but he stood up. Hesta kissed the palm of her hand and blew, like blowing a kiss to a child from a distance. But when she blew, a sound, low and harmonic, carried the kiss to Godwyn.

It was obvious that it worked. He dropped his hands and grinned. "Great Mother, that's better."

"I bet you still feel a bit thick in the head?" Hesta asked.

"A little," he admitted, "but after the thundering screech in my brain, anything is better."

"Excuse me, what was that?" Evie asked.

"A siren's kiss, of course," Godwyn replied.

Evie turned and stared at Hesta. "That's not the way I received my siren's kiss."

Hesta winked. "But yours was much nicer than one blown through the air. Admit it."

"I admit nothing. But it seems like you took advantage." Evie turned away and walked off.

Hesta reached out and stopped Evie before she got away. "No, stop. I'm sorry for teasing. The other way doesn't work with you. I tried, and it didn't work."

Evie stopped in her tracks. "You tried?"

"I did."

Evie stared at Hesta's face and looked for any signs of subterfuge. She saw none. "I'm sorry I doubted you."

"Quite all right. Now, shall we go and see what on this good earth is going on?"

16

They didn't have to go far, and every step was like walking through partly set toffee. Then it suddenly wasn't, the invisible impediment to progress lifted, and they walked as normal, at least for a while, until it returned in full force.

"Bloody hell," Evie said, and even the words struggled to come out of her mouth. "What is this? It's like a wall of nothingness made solid."

"Yes," Hesta agreed. But she added nothing more; instead she forced herself onwards.

"People ahead," Evie said, and tried to point, but the effort to raise her arm seemed far too great.

"Hesta, do something," Godwyn forced his words out.

Hesta stopped. "I'm a siren, not a sonos."

"That's close enough, Hesta, just do something!" Godwyn said.

"I don't know if I can." She stared at the ground for a moment as though inspiration might be found amidst the cobbles of the road.

"You can do this," Evie said.

Hesta held out her arms and forced Godwyn and Evie to

stand behind her. She took a deep breath and sang. If you could call the wave of sounds that came from her mouth a song. It started midrange, a single note that split into two, one higher and one lower, until the range of sound varied in undulating waves between a heart-bumping bass and up to a glass-shattering pitch.

Evie couldn't see anything, but the sound tore through her, and she feared her internal organs would try to move and change places. She reached for Hesta's hand, and the sound changed. She could almost see the wave of force that came from the song and rolled forward, moving all obstacles, seen and unseen, out of the way.

Hesta took a step forward. Godwyn and Evie followed, and it was as though Hesta had speared a path through the sound from the sonos. They could walk almost as normal now, and they made steady progress. Hesta kept her sounds local to them and bandied her gift as a shield of sound.

They were almost to the river. Along the street, the black shapes of the old shipyards rose out of the gloom. Here the sound stopped, and Hesta's countering wave raced further forward.

She stopped singing and took a moment to look at Evie and Godwyn. "It's stopped now. Are you all right?"

Evie nodded.

"Let's get on," Godwyn said gruffly.

At the end of the street, quite a crowd had gathered. Some stood around, shocked and disorientated. Others sat on the ground, and a few lay unmoving. Evie headed to the closest one, a woman of middle age, her salt-and-pepper hair spread over the ground like a fallen hood. Evie touched the woman's forehead and whispered. "It's all right now. Let me help." Then she extended her skill into the woman.

Evie grimaced as spikes of searing agony ripped through her head. She saw swelling that pressed against the inside of the skull, and it pulsed with a beat of its own.

"The brain is swollen," Evie said. *'I'm not sure what to do.'* She spoke directly to Hesta's mind. *'An infection would just come to me, but this is in her brain. I might damage her.'*

Hesta grabbed Evie's shoulder and squeezed her reassurance. *'She might die if you don't do something. How can you reduce the swelling?'*

"I don't know," Evie whispered.

She turned her attention to the next person, who looked in the worst condition. He also had a brain swollen and reddened, but less so. Her gift looked into his damage, and she saw how the fluids trapped and irritated the soft tissues there. Now she could see the differences, and her magic marked this as 'not-quite-right.'

She closed her eyes and allowed her gift-fired vision to center her inspection on all of those instances where the fluid gathered. She pulled them to herself until her mouth filled with the rancid stench of meat soaked in curdled milk. It took all of her self-control to stop herself from gagging.

Almost immediately, the swelling in his head lessened. Now she could apply this newfound knowledge to the worst sufferer: the woman.

The moment Evie's gift reached out, the pain the woman suffered drove through her own head. Without her gift, she'd never hope to manage the pain and do anything to help. Yet she managed to push through the agony and absorb that milk curdled meat flavor into her mouth. With it came the swelling from the woman's brain.

"I think you're helping," Hesta said.

The woman opened her eyes. "Thank you."

Evie nodded. She'd resolved the worst of the problem; she had to hope that nature would heal the rest. Or a medic if the woman could afford one.

Evie couldn't think about things like that, not right then. She had to move on to the next person. They all had headaches of some kind, but none had such a great swelling, and for that Evie was most grateful. She needed to help as many as she could. Nonetheless, she'd not even helped half a dozen when she accepted that she had done enough. Her hands had swollen so much that she couldn't move her fingers.

She stood up and stumbled against Hesta. "I need to…"

Before she knew it, Hesta and Godwyn had bundled her around a corner. "Do it here, it's clear," Hesta said.

Evie thought of all that she had absorbed, drew it together away from her hands, and vomited a stinking stream of liquid against the building. Hesta rubbed her back. "It's all right, Evie, I'm here."

She coughed a few times, but she'd ridded herself of as much as she could.

"We need to rethink this," Evie said. "Swallowing this much is likely to break me. The pain is almost more than I can bear. It's worse than anything."

"Then you have done enough," Hesta said.

"But there are more of them in pain, and I haven't really cured anything."

"They will be in more pain if we can't find the source of the problem."

They walked along the banks of the river, and wherever they went there were people who suffered.

"Don't stop," Godwyn said.

"Not unless they are really sick. We can always get them help later," Hesta said. "We need to get to the heart of it."

Hesta tucked her arm around Evie and ushered her along. All the way to the hall of the vitalists.

Outside, in the full shadow of Stake Island, Galeazzi Poul knelt on the ground with a young boy laid out beside him.

"He's trying to help with his skill. Is it a gift?" Hesta asked.

They reached Galeazzi, but he didn't look up. His attention seemed focused solely on the boy on the ground. He had one hand on the top of the boy's head and one on his chest.

Evie's gift flared. The boy had a weakness in his bones. Evie had seen this before from sailors, and in Bristelle there were a great many sailors. The boy had other weaknesses, too, but other than a tantalizing hint that they existed, she couldn't be certain what they meant.

She dropped to the ground opposite Galeazzi, put her hand on the boy's head, and moved Galeazzi's hands away from the boy's chest. "I'll heal, you revive, all right?" She didn't wait for his response but poured her gift and her will into the boy as fast as she could, and then pulled the swelling from his head. It rolled into her along with the other sicknesses she had not identified. But she didn't have the luxury of time to think things through, she had to act quickly.

When she had done all she could, she sat back on her heels and let Galeazzi take over. "Revive him," she said.

First of all, he altered the way the boy lay, then he pumped the boy's chest and breathed into his mouth a few times before repeating the pattern. Pump, breathe. Pump, breathe. He kept doing this over and over, and the whole time tears ran down Galeazzi's face.

Evie was about to tell him to give up, that it was too late, when the boy took a shuddering breath. Galeazzi grabbed the boy in his arms and crushed him to his chest. "Thank the Mother, and thank the Father. Blessed are we to be shown a miracle." Then he turned to Evie. "Thank you. Words can never repay you for this."

"No need," she said. "To see a life saved is payment enough. I would not have known how to revive him in that way. I should like to learn."

"Papa?" said the boy.

"Yes, son?"

"The pain is gone. Did you take it away?"

"No, son, this lady…" He looked up at her.

"Evie Chester," she answered the unspoken question.

Galeazzi smiled. "Evie Chester helped fix you."

The boy looked at Evie. Side by side, she could see the resemblance. The same dark eyes and dark hair, the high cheekbones and narrow face were too alike for them to be anything other than related. The boy could be no more than ten or eleven years old, but he held out his hand with the politeness of a gentleman. "Ajan Poul," he said. "Thank you."

Evie took his hand and shook lightly. "Glad to be of help. I hope your father will teach me a few things, so I can help more people."

"Papa likes to teach people, especially to help sick people," Ajan said.

"I do, and I'll teach Miss Chester. It's a promise," Galeazzi said.

"What do you know about the cause of this problem? Everyone here is sick," Evie said.

"I don't know. Someone came running into the hall saying they were being attacked by the gifted."

"Did you know the person?"

"No, never seen him before, but I see a great many people, and I can't always remember them. And when I'm performing, I focus on the task not the audience."

"I see." Evie looked into his eyes. "And do you believe in what you do?"

"Of course, I do! In fact, there is a demonstration at the university, three days hence, where they will see what I have to offer."

Godwyn helped Evie to her feet. "You do not look well at all." He touched her hand. "I think people need to settle down. The worst cases have been addressed, but you need to rest up."

"I can stand on my own now, I think, Godwyn," she said. "But you're right, I'm tired."

He nodded. "We should go home."

Godwyn and Hesta ushered her out of the crowds and part way down the street. "Now, purge before you split yourself in two," Godwyn said.

Evie didn't need to be told twice. She vomited all of the absorbed fluids and inflamed elements against the wall in one foul-smelling deluge. She wiped her mouth on her sleeve and said, "You know, Godwyn, it's bloody strange not to have you trying to put me in a pen with chains."

He shrugged. "Things change. I'm a practical man, and when there is a fork in the road, I like to think I'm wise enough to take the route that takes me where I want to go."

"Which is where?" Evie asked.

"Here," he answered.

"Do we need to have this discussion now?" Hesta asked.

"Yes," Evie said. "I wish to know why such a man as your brother is playing nursemaid to a woman like me."

"Power. I have power and influence, and now I wish for more." He grinned. "You were useful once. Now you shall be useful again, for me and for my sister."

Now she saw it. "You do know I don't trust you as far as I can spit fire, Bethwood," Evie said.

"You can trust me now. At least as long as you assist Hesta and don't get in the way of progress."

Evie nodded. "I think I can do that."

"Good. I believe it will be most equitable if that is so."

17

At a little before four in the afternoon that Sunday, Evie sat with Agatha and Florie in the parlour. They'd had lunch at the usual time, and now they sat in silence. Agatha read the paper, and Evie made marks on a small chalkboard. She was trying to write her name without it looking as though something had died and crossed the board with random smudges of chalk.

"I hope we'll be more chatty later," Florie said.

"We're thinking," Agatha said.

Evie smiled. "It is not necessary to fill the air with needless chatter all the time."

"Talking isn't needless," Florie said.

"It is if you have nothing useful to say," Agatha said.

"Quite right," Evie agreed.

"Have we got everything ready?" Florie asked.

"Sit down, Florie. You're making us nervous," Evie said.

Agatha looked over the top of her paper and snorted. "Patience, dear girl."

Florie slumped in her chair and glared at Evie.

"And you should sit upright, young lady," Agatha said. "Don't slouch."

Florie clicked her fingers together and a small flame appeared at the end of her thumb. She doused the flame and repeated the trick. Over and over.

"Florie," Evie said.

"I'm just—" A knock at the front door interrupted whatever she was about to say. "I'll get it," she said, and she rushed out of the room.

"Are you ready to check that this young man is suitable for our girl?" Agatha asked.

"Not really. How would I do that?"

"Let's see how it goes."

A bubble of chatter filled the hallway and spilled into the parlour. Evie tried to smile, but smiles were rare, especially when she had to meet a new person. It all seemed so serious.

Florie burst into the room and dragged a gangly young man behind her. He was tall, skinny, and looked all knees and elbows. He wore a suit, held his hat in his hand, and pulled at the cream silk cravat around his pale throat. He swallowed hard when Evie stared at him, and he ran his fingers through hair dark enough to be almost black.

"This is Simple," Florie said.

"Florie!" Agatha admonished. She folded the paper and put it to the side. "Come in, young man."

He stared at Evie as he entered the room. "Thank you, ma'am," he said. "I'm Simon. Pleased to make your acquaintance."

Evie stood up and gestured to one of the chairs. "Take a seat and make yourself comfortable, Simon. It's nice to meet one of Florie's friends." She smiled then. "Especially one who has taught her to use her skills and how to steal so well."

He gulped so hard his Adam's apple looked fit to burst from his throat. He stared at the ground and bobbed his head as though to lessen his height.

"Oh, don't you worry about Evie," Florie said. "She's soft, really."

Florie took his hat and put it in the hallway. He seemed lost without something to hold.

"Come sit, Simon, there's a chap. We'll not bite," Agatha said.

"Yes, ma'am," he said.

"How do you like your tea?" Agatha asked.

For the next hour they drank tea, ate sandwiches and cakes, and talked. Agatha and Evie grilled the young man about everything they could think of, and after a while he fielded the questions without getting embarrassed.

"Simon," Evie said. "I need your help."

"Of course," he answered.

"How good are you at finding things out?" she asked.

"Depends what you want to know."

"Have you heard anything about gifted people?"

He nodded. "I haven't heard much, but the Cainers have been getting sick, and they say the slave masters are using the gifted against them."

"That doesn't make sense," Evie said.

"I only know what I heard," he replied defensively.

Evie stopped for a moment. "Sorry, Simon, I wasn't questioning you. I just can't see why anyone would want to stir up the Cainers like this."

"Anything about vitalists?" Agatha added.

"Them mesmers?" he asked.

"Yes," Evie said.

"They say they can work magic that is not like the healers of the Towers or nuffink like that. It's magic of the Father," he said.

"And what do they say about it?"

He paused to think for a moment. "One of them, think it was the boss mesmer, he fixed Matthew Morrins' gout. And Petunia Davids, the one with the rheumatism of the knees, the other one fixed that and she swears she hasn't even got an ache anymore."

"Fascinating," Evie said.

"Best was when Annie the bonesetter fixed Alfred the ferryman's busted arm. He said they took the pain away and he felt nothing when Annie set it," he said.

"Now, that's something special," Agatha said.

"Is this all true?" Evie asked.

He shrugged. "I can find out more, if you like."

"Would you?" Evie asked.

"Sure would, if you think it's useful."

"It is. You know Florie and I are gifted, and you know where we have been kept, as well."

"I do," he said. "It wasn't right."

"You can see how we might be very sensitive to news and gossip that might make our lives difficult again."

"I wouldn't like that to happen to you either. I'll see what I can find. I have a couple of friends right in the heart of Cainstown. They'll know."

"Thank you, that would be much appreciated," Evie said.

Florie jumped to her feet. "Can we go out now?"

"Where to?" Agatha asked.

Simon stood up. "What we mean is, is it all right if I step out with Florie for a few hours? There is a tea house along the way, and it would be real nice to walk off this amazing tea time treat."

Agatha beamed at him. "Of course it's all right." She turned to Evie. "Isn't it?"

"Yes, it is. Go out. Be careful, and don't come back too late."

"We won't," Simon said.

Agatha waited until the front door slammed shut behind the two. "He's nice, isn't he?"

"I agree. I actually liked him, and I think he thinks the world of Florie."

"Can't ask any more of him, can we?"

"No," Evie agreed. "I am so glad that Florie can be happy, though. It takes a weight off my mind."

"And will you be happy?"

Evie shrugged. "Who's to say."

18

To the north of the city, between Queen's Park and the Badesville district, the huge municipal buildings of Bristelle dominated the landscape. City Hall, the Rotunda, the main university buildings, the hospital, and the asylum stood tall and pale against the darkness of Queen's Park. The afternoon sun sat low on the horizon, and Evie sat next to Hesta in the calash behind the hospital. The barrier across the road had yet to be raised.

"Are you sure we're allowed in?" Evie asked.

"Yes."

"But women aren't permitted. Even if Galeazzi put in a good word for us, he wouldn't have that much influence at the university."

"Normally you would be correct and we'd be refused access to the hallowed hall of the medics, but there are many benefits to a brother who knows so many people."

"Really?"

"In the city, political influence is all that matters, and these days Godwyn has plenty," Hesta said.

Evie had a fair idea how Godwyn had gathered his

influence, and most of it probably involved keeping his mouth shut.

"They're expecting us and will not deny us access," Hesta said.

"Then why are we waiting here?" Evie asked.

"Waiting for the porter to raise the barrier." Hesta pointed to the circular building off to the side. "That's the Rotunda, where they run their medical lectures and demonstrations, or whatever they're called."

Evie nodded. She stared out towards the Rotunda as an old fellow wearing a long coat and hat strode towards them. Like many municipal porters, he was old enough that his grey hair had almost turned white and stuck out from under his hat in a cloud. As he drew closer, more details could be seen. His long black coat had burgundy sleeve cuffs and lapels, just like the doorman at one of the fancy hotels.

He raised his hat as he approached. "Miss Bethwood and Miss Chester?"

"Yes," Hesta answered.

He pointed towards the Rotunda, a circular building with small single-storey annexes joined to the central building. "Take the carriage around the back to disembark, and then your driver needs to find a space back here to wait. There are many others to arrive, but the carriage park is already full. It looks like this is a very popular demonstration."

"Got that, Charlie?" she asked.

Charlie raised his hat. "Yes, Miss Bethwood. And I will be ready to pick you up when you've finished."

"Thank you, Charlie," Evie said.

Dozens of carriages lined the coach park, and men in fine suits loitered about the back of the building. They were most boisterous and loud in their discussions, until Hesta and Evie's carriage pulled up to the front steps. The men stopped talking and stepped away from the carriage, as if being a woman might be considered contagious.

A porter, dressed much like the one at the barrier, strode out of the main doors. He flapped his hands about as though to fend off a feminine assault. "Excuse me, this is an area restricted to invitation and appointment only."

Out of the crowd, like the proverbial bad penny, strode Godwyn himself. "Excuse me, good fellow, these two ladies are expected."

"But—"

"No buts, dear chap, open the door and help them out of the carriage." Godwyn waved his hands about in the same overly dramatic fashion as the porter had and opened the door for them himself. He lowered the mounting step and held out his hand.

Hesta left first. "Thank you, Godwyn."

Evie followed, but she didn't touch Godwyn's hand. "Thank you," she said.

"This is most irregular," the porter insisted.

Godwyn stared at the man.

"Most irregular," the porter repeated. "I would have to have a word with the Dean of Medics."

"Good," Godwyn said. "There he is. Looks like he's coming outside and heading here now." He raised his hand. "Doctor Montgomery, Joym, good to see you again. Come join us, my dear fellow, and let me introduce you."

The porter stared at the doctor. "Dean Montgomery, you will permit women inside the building? There are no facilities. Nothing."

"It's fine," Joym said "It is my responsibility."

"As you wish, sir," the porter said, and walked away, muttering and shaking his head.

"This is my sister, Hesta, and her companion, Miss Evie Chester."

Joym nodded to them both. "Ladies. I'm pleased to make your acquaintance. Now, you are aware that these halls are generally not suitable for ladies, and sometimes the demonstrations can be quite unpalatable, perhaps even quite vulgar, to the more delicate feminine disposition."

Evie narrowed her eyes; she could show him a thing or two about unpalatable.

"We're not at all squeamish, I can assure you," Hesta said before Evie could add something.

He nodded. "Then perhaps now is the time to go inside before all the space is taken by the students and others interested in today's demonstration."

"Perhaps we should," Hesta agreed. She smiled, too, and that seemed to disarm the chap.

"Then if you would be so good as to come this way, I'll show you to the hall." He pulled his shoulders back and gestured towards the building. At the heart rose the circular walls of the Rotunda, but one of the square annexes had become an entrance hall.

There were people—no, men—everywhere, and when Hesta and Evie approached, the men ceased talking to watch them pass by.

Through the hallway, door porters opened a set of double doors, and a wall of sound rolled out from the multi-tiered Rotunda hall. It was laid out like a theatre, with ascending circles of seating all the way around the room. To left and right of the doors, steps led up to the tiers, each with a chest-high rail. Each of the tiers were full of men talking loudly enough that they might be heard over the other conversations.

"This way," Joym said. He continued forward and led them to the lowest tier. Godwyn entered the tier first and made sure they had enough room.

"Excellent," he said. "Many thanks."

Joym nodded. "Enjoy the demonstration."

Evie took a deep breath. There were so many people, and the cacophony of voices set her teeth on edge. But that was not as worrisome as the hush that fell over the room as the men in the audience realised there were women present.

The silence could only be described as unnatural.

Godwyn rapped his knuckles on the wooden shelf of the rain. "Gentlemen, please, even you must have seen a woman before. As you were. This is a lecture and demonstration, and we're not yet in the morgue."

Bit by bit, the noise levels rose, but not to the levels they'd been.

When the curtains around the room were drawn closed and the light dimmed, small lamps around the demonstration area sprang into life and filled the center of the room with a pale glow.

19

E vie scrutinised the open area. It was laid out in exactly the same way as the vitalist performance had been. Two chairs and the half barrel contraption. She couldn't recall what it was called, exactly.

For the first part of the demonstration, Galeazzi used the same young woman he'd used before. She wondered about that. Galeazzi was one step ahead of her; as he went through his opening statements, he added a little more detail.

"Some people have seen this demonstration elsewhere. If I were them, then I might wonder why we use the same woman, Alice, for each demonstration."

Evie nodded to herself.

"It is a simple case of pragmatism. Alice has been a patient of mine for a long time, and so we have built up a good rapport and, more importantly, a degree of trust. I have helped her work through several issues, and although this is an ongoing process, Alice shows us how this whole process might work. Furthermore, mesmerism could readily expose a person's innermost secrets and worries, and I'm loath to allow such a thing to be done to a stranger in a public way."

Evie found herself nodding to that, too.

"My colleague, Ekvard Halms, will demonstrate the use of mesmerism not just for the treatment of the mind, but as a tool to aid healing of the body. This particular part of the demonstration can only be seen here and no place else. Enjoy, and welcome to the world of mesmerism, animal magnetism, and vitalism."

The rest of this part of the demonstration was pretty much as they had already seen. Evie searched the audience, at least the people she could see, for any sign of someone acting in a suspicious way. Hesta did the same.

No one stood out. The men were very interested in the demonstration and that was where the focus of their attention lay.

Galeazzi used another young man to demonstrate the way that the mesmerist could control pain. As with the previous performance, this man did not even flinch when they stuck him with a needle. Several needles.

Even though she had already seen this done, Evie could not understand how anyone could control pain in quite that way.

Galeazzi explained the stored magnetism of the barrel setup and gave a run-through of the device in operation. He did not call for people to use the equipment. "Later, if you wish to experience the buquette, then I will be available at the end. Right now, if you need a break, this is the time to take five minutes. In the meantime, we need to move a few things in preparation for our next demonstration." He looked at the watch from his pocket. "Five minutes, gentlemen." He looked up at Evie and Hesta. "And ladies."

Porters in the uniform of the university arrived to remove the equipment in the center of the room and replace it with different equipment: two trolleys with trays of implements, a trolley covered with white linens, and two aprons.

"What's this?" Evie asked. "This was not a part of the demonstration before."

"No, I know. He said the next part would be different to what we have seen. Do you need a break before it starts?"

Evie shook her head. "I'm too busy looking for problems. Have you seen anything?"

"No. You?"

"Nothing. Maybe there is nothing here to see."

"Do you really believe that?"

"No."

20

A fter their break, the men of the audience shuffled in with hardly a word. A sense of expectation filled the room. Evie wondered if many of the attendees had already seen the first part, and now the chance to see something new filled them with the need to know, to see the magic of the sciences in action.

They didn't have long to wait. Galeazzi strode into the room and waited for people to settle into stillness before he spoke.

"Gentleman, and ladies, this is the most important part of the demonstration, insofar as this esteemed establishment is concerned." He chose then to walk around the room so he could address them all. "Fellow medics, in all surgeries there are two vital parts to the procedure that will determine if the patient makes a recovery or not. One of those is the chance of infection, and there are ways to keep those risks down."

Around the auditorium there were nods and murmurs of agreement. They were listening very closely to this. Evie was, too. Anything that involved infections always caught her attention.

"But there is one part of the procedure that defies control

and is, as often as not, the reason the patient does not recover. What do you suppose that might be?" Galeazzi asked. Before anyone could speak, he answered the question himself. "The use of soporifics is as deadly to a surgical patient as the shock of surgery itself and the threat of post-surgical infection. Gentlemen, there is an alternative. Let me introduce you to my surgical expert, from the university hospital of East Karnstem—Ekvard Halms." He raised his arm to draw attention to one of the other entrances.

Ekvard wore a dark but muted green suit that hung from his shoulders as though intended for someone with a much larger frame. He walked with a slight limp, and the cane he used in his left hand was not intended for show, as he leaned heavily upon it.

Evie guessed that Ekvard was much older than Galeazzi, at least from the thinning gray of his hair and the ragged wrinkles of his face and jowls.

"Good evening, gentlemen and fellow medics of Bristelle. As my colleague has mentioned, I am a surgeon, and I have performed in some of the most prestigious of hospitals in all of Eropea. It is not a boast but a matter of record that speaks of nothing more than the experience I have gained."

Evie stared at him. There was something unusual and elusive about him, but she couldn't see what it was. Her gift seemed to sleep. "Hesta," she whispered.

"Yes?" Hesta spoke into her ear as though she breathed the word.

Evie shivered at the feel of her warm breath on her neck. She almost forgot what it was she wanted to say. "I can't sense anything."

"Then be careful."

"Surgery," Ekvard continued, his voice louder, "is a dangerous thing. A very dangerous thing. But without it, our world would be littered with needless death." He gestured to the side and four porters carried in a table.

"For your edification, this evening we will perform a simple surgery, and I will prove that the use of soporifics is not necessary."

Another porter pushed a man in a wheelchair into the room and left the patient next to the table.

"Stand up, please," Ekvard said to the young man. When he did, the surgeon pulled up the patient's shirt to show a growth that had sprouted from the side of his ribcage. "This is Philip, and he has been affected by this growth for some years. It is my intention to remove this growth here in this theatre. Who would like to assist?"

From the roar of sound, every man attending the demonstration was eager to participate. Ekvard pointed to two people. "You and you, come forward and wash your hands, please, in the disinfectant provided."

He turned his attention to his patient and smiled. "Thank you for permitting us to perform this surgery. Please come and sit on the table."

"What happens now?" the man asked.

"I take this monstrosity from you," Ekvard said. "And no, it won't hurt at all."

Philip moved to the table and sat on the edge. Ekvard placed one hand on Philip's head and another on his chest.

"Sleep," Ekvard said. No sooner had he finished than Philip slipped to his side and the assistants laid him down. "Prepare him for surgery," he said to the two volunteers. "Now, I have told him to sleep because many patients find that the idea of watching themselves being cut is a little too much. But I shall make him look up when we are nearly done so you might see, with your own eyes, that he has not been given anything to make him sleep. Just the power of vitalism and a mesmer. With more time, I could make sure he felt no worries about the knife at all, and we could perform this entire surgery with his eyes open."

Evie almost jumped when Hesta grabbed her arm.

"I'm not sure I want to see this," Hesta whispered.

"You must. There is something here, I can feel it."

Evie reached out to touch Godwyn, who was staring at the process in the middle of the room with total focus.

"Godwyn," she whispered.

He stared at her for a moment, and then he blinked. "Evie?"

She gestured so that he leaned towards her. "Something feels wrong, Godwyn."

He nodded. "Understood."

It was as she spoke that Evie paid attention to the others. All, without exception, were focussed on Ekvard, and it seemed they were just a little too focussed. Of all the people in the room, only she, Godwyn, and Hesta were looking at anyone or anything other than the man in the middle of the room.

She turned her attention to Hesta. "Look at me." She gestured to her face, and Hesta stared into her eyes. Evie concentrated hard so she could speak to Hesta's mind. *'I think something strange is going on. I have never seen such a large group pay so much attention to one man.'*

'Yes. I agree, there is a sound, too…' Hesta's thoughts replied. *'I hear something, but I'm not sure what I'm hearing.'*

Evie focussed now on the proceedings in the center of the room. Ekvard and the volunteers had washed their hands, removed their jackets, and donned surgical aprons that seemed more suited to a butcher's shop than an operating room.

"I shall make a wide incision under the tumor and open a flap of skin. We'll see what this growth is and remove it. Then we'll end by sewing him back together. Are we ready, gentlemen?"

"Yes," replied the audience in unison, as though they had one voice.

That didn't seem right at all.

Hesta stared forward. *'He's a siren!'* she thought to Evie.

'But he's not singing.'

'Maybe he can't. Maybe he just enthralls with his voice when he talks?'

'You don't know?'

Hesta shook her head slowly.

Ekvard didn't wait. He sliced into Philip's side, and blood dripped from the table to the floor. As he cut, he continued to speak and gave a running commentary of every move, interspersed with instructions to his assistants.

"There. We see the tumour." He touched Philip on the shoulder. "You will wake up on the count of five. One," Ekvard said. "When you wake up, you will be fully awake and not in the slightest bit sleepy. Two. You will feel no pain. Three. You will show no concern for what we are doing. Four. You will be happy and refreshed from this brief sleep. Five." He snapped his fingers.

Philip opened his eyes. "Hello, doctor, did the surgery go well?"

"We're still in the middle of it. But so far, everything is good." Ekvard returned to the process of removing the growth. He addressed the audience again. "As you can see, using this procedure not only negates the use of soporifics, but we can reduce surgical trauma and work much faster. The sooner we have the issue resolved and the patient sewn up, the sooner they can heal and with fewer risks."

Evie couldn't see the surgery itself, but she heard the sound of something wet as Ekvard dropped it in a bowl.

"And there it is, all gone." He turned to the assistants. "You can sew him up. Make the stitches nice and tight, as he will be up and walking very soon."

Philip groaned on the table.

"What's the matter?" Ekvard asked, his voice as sharp and as pointed as a blade.

"I feel sick, doctor."

"Sick?" Ekvard sounded incensed that anyone would have the audacity to be sick on his table. He pressed his patient backward. "Philip, listen to my voice. You feel nothing. How do you feel?"

"Nothing," Philip replied.

"You are well. It is the sight of the surgery which causes your untrained mind to fret. Isn't that true?"

"It is true."

"Surgery is complex, and too much for you to comprehend at this moment. But it won't last long. As soon as we have finished, we'll have a cup of tea and a slice of bread. What do you think to tea, Philip?"

"Tea sounds lovely."

"Then it won't be long," Ekvard said. He looked around the room but focused his attention away from Evie to the other side. He spoke with passion about mesmerism and then returned to the surgical table.

"This, gentlemen, is the application of the scientific method, and we are making great strides. Beware of the witches of Towers and other places who make claims based on dark magic dark which has no place under the scientific light." He turned back to Philip, checked the stitches, and pronounced that the work was fine and sound.

He held out his hand. "Sit up, Philip. There is no pain any more, is there?"

"No, sir, no pain."

The assistants helped him to stand upright.

"This, gentlemen, is the way surgery should be. Safe. Fast. Effective. Thank you."

Philip wobbled a little on his feet, and Ekvard held out a hand. "Steady on. With all the weight we removed from your side, you are probably feeling lopsided."

The men in the audience laughed at the joke. Then they clapped and cheered with great and enthusiastic merriment.

That's when the illusion slipped for Evie, and her gift gave her a brief glimpse into the true nature of the problem.

Something, a black and oily something, had wrapped itself around Ekvard. It wavered in and out of her vision, but there was no denying the presence of the bulbous body that clung to the man's back. Tentacles wafted in the air around Ekvard, several smaller ones not only touched his head and neck but disappeared inside. Others vanished into his back, arms, and legs. It was as though the creature wore Ekvard like some demonic glove puppet. The creature wavered and vanished for a moment, only to reappear again as tentacles stretched from the doctor to Philip.

Philip stumbled forward. Blood seeped down his side where the less than perfect stitches had puckered open. She could see infection already rolling through the wound, eating away at healthy skin and spreading throughout his body.

Tentacles reached out and held the surgical cut closed. Something else, a different kind of infection, seeped into Philip's skin. Drops of oily corruption burrowed into him.

No one else could see this. At least, Evie assumed they couldn't see it. If they could, they would scream and shout. Instead, the gentlemen and the medics present did no more than sound their applause in rousing and enthusiastic fashion.

Evie knew exactly what this was. *'Demon!'* she shrieked into Hesta's mind. But it wasn't that Ekvard was a demon; the demon had attached to him. *'Ekvard is possessed.'*

'What? Possessed by what kind of demon?' Hesta asked.

"I don't know. It is a slimy tentacled thing," she whispered to Hesta. "The audience is enthralled, but the demon can't control as the entire room and keep itself hidden at the same time. The illusion slipped, and now I know how to see beyond this magic."

Hesta stared forward. "I can't see—"

Evie felt the excitement rise within her. "It's my gift to see what has no place here. I see it!"

"What should I do?"

"Can you un-enthrall the people here?"

"I can't do anything like that."

"Give them all a siren's kiss or something," Evie suggested.

"It would take too..." Hesta didn't finish. She paused for a moment, as though in deep thought, and then she opened her mouth and a high-pitched shriek nearly blew Evie's ears off. Pain flashed through her head and then diminished as quickly as it had arisen. The undulating wail continued, and with it came a sense of absolute terror. For a moment, fear gripped Evie's heart so intensely it almost stopped beating. Then the terror loosened its grip on her insides and she took deep gulps of air to steady herself.

Evie stared at Hesta as she sang. The protection she expected from the siren's kiss almost didn't work. But then, the song that came from Hesta's mouth was an unpleasant and nerve-grating screech.

It worked, though. Men all around the room started to waken. The noise of the room rose from the silent attention given to the surgery into something else. The audience was like a beast wakening from a nightmare. Their feet shuffled about as they got their bearings, their breaths grew louder, more laboured.

"Stop," Evie hissed, "before they panic."

Too late. A wall of cries and screams rose from the audience. Fear fed fear.

"I can't stop them now."

Hesta's song changed, soothing nerves instead of inspiring horror. Evie could hear the difference. But it was too late, the crowd had turned into a terrified mob.

Godwyn swept the three of them together and pushed

them against the barrier, using his body as a shield. Men scrambled and bellowed in terror and rising anger.

"We have to get to Ekvard," Evie said, her voice muffled under Godwyn's bulk.

"Wait," he said.

They were jostled and kicked. Someone jumped on them, and Godwyn grunted with the pain. Throughout it all, he remained stalwart and strong. When he released them, the theatre was empty. The surgical equipment had been tipped over and some of the barriers between the tiers had been ripped up. Shards of wood lay everywhere.

Godwyn straightened up and helped Evie and Hesta to stand. "What the hell is going on?"

"We need to get out of here first," Evie said. "And then plan."

21

They gathered themselves in the drawing room at Bethwood House, Hesta's new home. Evie sat on one end of the couch, a cup of cooling tea in her hand. Hesta sat at the other end and stared at the stove. Godwyn sat in the armchair, his gaze fixed on the sideboard on the opposite side of the room. For a group that was usually so chatty, no one seemed capable of talking at all.

Evie sipped at her cooling tea. "I saw it," she said.

"What exactly did you see?" Godwyn asked.

She looked up to see the man she had grown to hate leaning forward in his seat. He actually wanted to know. He'd protected her. Hesta as well, but that he'd shielded them both at the same time didn't fit with the monster she knew. What had happened in the world to turn him into this person? She had no illusions about what he was like, and she couldn't see him as the caring type. But he'd changed, a little at least, and wasn't the man he had been. She shrugged off the thought. People didn't change.

Evie did her best to explain everything from the moment the surgical demonstration had started. She tried to tie in her observations with the events as Godwyn and Hesta perceived them so they could all understand how the events had unfolded.

"I saw nothing other than the surgery," Godwyn said, "and what I saw looked fine. More than fine."

"Illusion," Evie said.

"How did you feel whilst you were watching the surgery?" Hesta asked.

He inhaled deeply, as though the question forced him to reconsider the whole of the evening. "It was a fascinating thing to watch. But I couldn't shake off the feeling that something wasn't right," he admitted. "Towards the end, I felt this surge of fear." He paused. "Not fear, terror. Just before the chaps all went wild, there was a sharp pain in my head, too."

"That was Hesta," Evie said.

Godwyn turned to his sister. "You?"

"I had to try to counter the siren effect from Ekvard," Hesta said. She turned to Evie. " Is he really a siren though?"

"I don't know," Evie replied. She thought back to the start of the song. "You do know that when you start to use your voice, we don't always hear or recognise what's going on?"

"I think so." Hesta sounded uncertain.

"Does your kiss protect us only from your voice or from all sirens?"

"I'm not sure," Hesta said.

Evie scrutinised her face. "You don't know much about being a siren, do you?"

"In the same way you don't know everything about being a syphon."

Evie shrugged. "Until I met you, I was quite happy being a healer of sickness. It's a skill to be proud of."

"My gift didn't appear until I became a woman. Not long after I started experimenting with my gift, I met someone…" Hesta's voice drifted off. "That's when I became cursed. My voice came and went with the healing and attentions of the gifted. But it never lasted long. Every time it did, the messenger would come back and strengthen the curse."

"Until I came along and cured your throat and took care of the demon?"

Hesta nodded. "So my knowledge of my own skills is perhaps less than you imagine. I've not really had it that long."

"You hinted as much when you read from your book. Not to worry, we'll discover who we both are, as we go along," Evie said. She paused. "I noticed the first time I heard you sing that it was as though you made the audience love you."

"I did?" Hesta looked thoughtful. "I suppose I do. Although I prefer to think that I help them experience the emotion of the songs."

"Well, you sang the audience tonight into a state of terror."

"Girls!" Godwyn exclaimed. "Never mind a discussion of sirens or syphons, or whatever. We've other concerns to deal with. Like the events at the university. Are you sure it was a demon?"

Evie glared at him.

He held his hands in the air. "All right, all right. It's just a lot to take in. And there will be repercussions."

"Such as?" Hesta asked.

"I doubt the university will accept the destruction of so much property in a near riot," Evie said.

"Indeed, Evie has the right of it," Godwyn agreed. "Although the degree of fuss will depend on who was there. Certain families have a habit of making distasteful events disappear."

"Never mind the fancy families, we need to find Ekvard, or the patient. I don't think he will live long if someone doesn't get to him soon."

"Right, Of course." Godwyn stroked his chin thoughtfully.

"You have an idea?' Hesta asked.

"I do. All that remains is to work out who was the most important person there."

"And then what?" Evie asked.

"Call the constabulary and complain to the Dean of the medics, of course," he said.

"What will that do?" Hesta asked.

"They will be so busy chasing the cause of the riot that I'm sure the dean will be more than eager to help us look for the patient."

"If he is in the hospital," Evie said.

"Where else would you put a sick man?"

"It's too late for start tonight, Godwyn. We shall do this first thing in the morning." Hesta turned to Evie. "You should stay here with us in the spare room. It's not the finest of rooms, but it's warm and clean."

"I really need to go home, Agatha—Mrs. Hickman will be worried," Evie said.

Godwyn shook his head and crossed the room to the door in three quick strides. "Nonsense. Stay here where it is safer for you, and safer for them, too. I'll get runners out. Sit, relax, eat something if you can. It's going to be a long night."

22

L ater that evening, much later, a knock at the front door announced the arrival of Inspector Willis of the Bristelle City Constabulary.

Godwyn went to let him in and ushered the inspector into the drawing room. He came alone, though. Evie had expected to see a couple. After all, they always seemed to go everywhere in pairs.

"Inspector, this is Hesta Bethwood, my sister, and her friend and associate, Evie Chester. They were both present when the chaps grew quite *boisterous*." He stressed the word so much no one could take it as anything other than an understatement.

The inspector bowed perfunctorily. "It is my understanding that women are not allowed into the Rotunda theatre."

"Generally not, but these are ladies of a medical interest, and the dean permitted them for the demonstration."

"I see," he said.

"I have already informed the Dean of Medics about the demonstration. I think that some recompense for the behaviour of these so-called gentlemen is in order."

"Of course, Mr Bethwood, but you know how young men can be."

"Yes, and they nearly killed these two ladies here."

Willis stiffened. "Do you wish to make a complaint about these gentlemen?"

"I do," Godwyn said.

"Do you happen to know who was there?"

"Dear fellow, there were almost a hundred people present. I can't recall them all. However, the porters would."

"Do you recall any of their names?" Willis asked. From his pocket, he withdrew a notebook and a pencil. "Any details would be useful."

"Right," Godwyn said.

A feral grin lit his face as he started to list names. The inspector wrote down the first few and then stopped.

"Should I say them more slowly?" Godwyn asked.

"No. That's not necessary. I get the idea," Willis said. "I would like to speak to the dean, though, and get his thoughts on the matter."

"Just so, Inspector," Godwyn said.

"I understand he is on evening rounds in the hospital and cannot be contacted for a short while. There are patients who are in much need of care. I will speak with him first thing of the morning."

"The dean actually works at the hospital as well as running the university?" Evie asked.

"Yes, ma'am. It is a teaching hospital, and he likes to personally ensure the medics have performed well each day. He can't be contacted while on rotation."

"That is understandable," Godwyn said. "If you need us to make a statement, I'm at your disposal."

Willis bowed again. "Thank you, Mr Bethwood. I'll be in touch."

Godwyn led him to the door, and after a brief chat that Evie couldn't hear, he returned to Hesta and Evie.

"Well, that wasn't much use, was it?" Evie said.

"On the contrary, it was very useful. It means that the police have no interest, and we know where the dean is. Shall we go and have a word?"

"You don't sound surprised," Hesta said.

Godwyn rolled his shoulders. "Do you think any officer of the law is going to take to task any of the young men associated with Bristelle's most important families? I suspect they are making a deposit to the university fund as we speak. By the end of the week, the Rotunda will look as good as new." Godwyn looked at his time piece. "Let's give them a short while to think about how they'll brush this under the rug."

"I think they've had enough time," Evie said. "Let's get going."

"But it's late," Hesta said.

"The dean will be at the hospital, and I doubt that he will make it a fast visit. It's worth a visit," Evie said.

Godwyn grinned. "I'll get the carriage."

23

B ristelle Infirmary and Centre for Medicine was a large building, four floors high, not including a basement, and large enough to take the space of dozens of houses. It presented a front of red-brick modern architecture, with little charm other than the ornamental and decorative window arches. A covered portico to the front allowed carriages to unload next to the door whilst remaining protected from the elements. And in Bristelle, the elements often meant rain.

Dim light seeped out from most of the windows on the top two floors, and only a few from the lower storeys.

The carriage stopped at the front of the hospital, under the portico, and waited. Godwyn grabbed a leather bag and jumped out. He offered his hand to Hesta and then to Evie. "Here we go."

"Isn't this a bit obvious? Maybe we should sneak in around back. They'll refuse us entry, surely," Evie said.

"Generally, yes," Godwyn agreed. "But it's late, so there's less staff present and no one knows who anyone is. Act as if you belong and leave the talking to me."

Evie had never been inside a hospital. There had never

been any need for her, and few gifted were ever invited inside one, unless they were from the Towers.

A porter in a pale grey uniform with burgundy sleeve cuffs caught their attention as soon as they entered the large entrance hall. The reception desk, off to one side, looked closed.

"Good evening," Godwyn said.

"Nurses are busy at this time, unless it is an emergency," the porter said.

"Well, I don't need a nurse. I'm late." He pulled out his fob watch from his waistcoat as though to emphasize the point. "Joym, I mean Doctor Montgomery, is expecting me. It never bodes well when someone is late, does it? Still travel is as it is, and when there are delays, what can you do?"

"Nothing," the porter agreed.

"I hope he didn't wait too long?" Godwyn asked.

The porter shrugged.

"Where is he? We'll catch up to him, and I'm sure our baggage will find us at some point."

"I understand. He's on his rounds. I expect he'll be in the long-term wards on the top floor." He pointed to the far wall. "Stairs are that way. Unless you want to wait for him until he finishes?"

"Most kind, but we'd best not wait. I don't want to annoy the dean any more than I probably already have," Godwyn said. He strode towards the stairs, with Hesta and Evie behind. As they went through the doors, he grumbled to himself loudly enough for Evie to hear. "Top floor, dammit. Why aren't the sick people on the ground floor? Or why isn't there some kind of lift? Then we have to start at the top," he said much louder. "Oh well. Up we go."

On the top floor, they strode through the interlinked wards as though they belonged there. No one paid them any attention, even when they pushed through each of the double doors that led from one ward to another. The beds were all full, forty to a ward and not a single spare bed between them.

Every now and then, Evie's gift flared up. "He's sick," she said.

"Of course, they're sick. This is a hospital," Godwyn said.

"But—"

"We don't have time," he interrupted.

"You can come back later," Hesta suggested.

Evie nodded. None of the people she saw could be considered terminal. "All right, then. Later. But I must come back."

They found Doctor Montgomery on the floor below. He'd just entered a ward that not only had a set of double doors but possessed a section separated by a glass screen. On the wall behind the door were pegs with thick and waxed smock tops and several full-face plague masks that made the medics look like strange birds.

Evie looked through the glass into the heart of the ward. There were fewer beds here and each one had been separated from its fellows by a thick curtain. Even so, one detail stood out more than any other: infection. Every single bed contained a person suffering from some sickness.

At the first bed, two plague-masked people attended the pale occupant lying between them. Evie knew that this was one who would not last the night. His body was almost consumed with darkness and burned in a failing attempt to keep the corruption at bay.

"I don't think you want to go in there," Evie said. She picked up one of the plague masks. "This isn't for show. Everyone in there is infected."

"With plague?" Godwyn asked.

Evie stared back through the window at the beds closest. "I don't know what they have, but they don't all suffer from the same condition. I'll know more when I get closer." She hoped so. In most cases, she knew no more than whether something was there. It was usually enough.

"Plague, Evie? You shouldn't expose yourself to such sickness," Hesta said.

"I must. It's what I do." She pointed along the ward. "Our patient is there, almost at the other end of the room."

Hesta looked where she pointed. "How can you tell? I can't see anyone."

"I can. I can see the sickness. Worse, I can sense something else."

"Something unnatural?"

Evie nodded. "I'm going inside. I need to help them all, if I can."

"Then we'll watch," Godwyn said.

Hesta reached out and touched Evie's arm before she could go through the glass door into the ward. "What if you get sick?"

"I won't."

"If I got sick, could you heal me?"

"Probably."

"Then I'm coming with you," Hesta said.

"You shouldn't."

Hesta looked into her eyes and wouldn't look away. "You might need me. You can heal me if I get sick."

Evie thought to protest, but gave in. "All right, then." She opened the door and stepped into the ward. She didn't bother with any of the protective clothing. She didn't need it, after all.

The two plague doctors nearest rushed to stop them. They spoke, but Evie couldn't understand what they said.

"I'm sorry, those masks make it hard to follow what you are saying."

One of them waved his hands about in a most dramatic fashion and tried to push her towards the glass anteroom. "You have to leave," a man said. Probably the doctor.

"No." Evie pointed to the man in the bed they'd stood by. "He's not going to last the night."

The plague doctor shook his head.

"I can help," Evie said. "But the person I need to see most of all is the patient who Ekvard operated on earlier."

That request stopped him.

"Evie, show him what you can do to help this man here, and then maybe we can have a talk outside," Hesta suggested.

Evie nodded, and so did the plague doctor. "You need to tell me what his sickness is," she said.

The other plague doctor lifted the sheets so Evie could see the blackened stump of the patient's leg. She called to her gift so she could check the flow of the infection.

"Gangrene?" she asked.

The doctor nodded, and she could just hear the muffled "Yes."

"It was left too long unseen and untreated?"

He nodded again. "Yes."

She stared at the wounds and the corruption within the patient's body and started to memorise the details and the effects. She would recognise this if she saw it again. Given enough time and knowledge, she was sure she'd know what to do each and every time. In this case, the start point seemed obvious.

"Pull the curtains around us," Evie instructed. "You can watch, but never repeat what you have seen. Will you agree to that?"

The two plague doctors nodded.

"Good. I also need a bucket," Evie said. She didn't wait to see of anyone fulfilled her instructions. As soon as the curtains closed, she stood next to the patient in his bed. She smoothed the wet hair from his blazing hot forehead, opened his damp pyjamas, and lifted the coverings from his leg. She closed her eyes and laid a hand on his chest and the other inches above the ravaged edges of his stump.

The sickness rolled into her in waves with such speed that her hands turned black and were soon covered in pustules. The pustules didn't stay long, vanishing almost as soon as they formed. She sucked in as much of his corruption as she could and then turned away. "Don't touch me," she warned them, and shied away when Hesta came too close.

The doctor offered her a bowl, which she accepted. "Another one as well," she said, and vomited a spew of stinking black slime almost thick enough to be called tar. Within the black, she could see globules of yellow and red. Worst of all was the stink and the taste that coated her mouth.

One of the doctors started to retch.

"Get away if you can't cope with this," she said. Then she handed the full bowl to the doctor and placed the empty one at her feet on the floor. She still had so much to get rid of. It swelled into her fingers, and the sides of her nails split. Pus collected together and dripped into the metal bowl with a steady *plink*.

Someone offered her a metal cup. Inside she could see nothing more than water. She took a mouthful, sloshed it around her mouth, and spat it into the bowl. "How is he?"

The doctor examined the patient and nodded. "Much better. How—"

"Don't ask," Evie interrupted. She considered healing him more, but then she thought she might need her energy for later. "Let's talk," she said, and left the ward.

The first of the gowned plague doctors removed his mask as soon as he entered the antechamber. A hot and florid Doctor Montgomery stared at the three of them. "Godwyn, what the devil are you all doing here?"

"I came to find you. What's the dean of the university doing working the rounds?"

"I prefer to be here rather than doing the paperwork from

the Rotunda incident. I have staff who do that better than I can."

"Good man. I would do the same in your shoes," Godwyn said.

"Anyway," he gestured to the women, "what are they doing here?"

"Joym, you've met them both," Godwyn said.

"Have I?"

"Earlier today before the demonstration," Godwyn said.

"Ahh, yes." He inclined his head towards Hesta and Evie. "So I did, but it has been a busy evening. And it was an eventful demonstration, I understand."

"Did you not attend yourself?" Godwyn asked.

"Goodness, no. Someone has to be here when all the medics are at the hall. Besides I've seen the demonstration before. Not at the university, mind, but elsewhere."

"About the demonstration, have you heard anything about what happened?" Godwyn asked.

"There was a damned riot, that's what I heard. There are six patients on the ground floor with crush injuries and minor cuts and abrasions. One has a splinter the thickness of his wrist sticking out of his side. What happened?"

Evie pointed down the ward. "That chap down there was the patient."

"Yes," Joym said. "He got injured in the crush."

"Oh, I think there is rather a lot more wrong with him than riot damage," Evie said. "Else he'd not be up here, yes?"

"Someone please tell me what the devil is going on!" Joym demanded.

"Let me explain," Hesta said.

As she spoke, Evie felt the delicate tickle of her gift brushing against her ears.

"The chaps at the demonstration were struck by some kind of great malaise," Hesta said. "Triggered, I think, by the sight of a patient undergoing surgery without the use of pain relief or soporifics. I'm surprised you did not stop to see such a thing."

Joym looked confused for a moment. "These shows are always the same, I think. I've never heard nor seen much in the way of surgery at the shows before."

Hesta nodded. "Nonetheless, it caused great distress, and the chaps were most aggressive when they tried to escape. That might be the cause of the injuries."

"Of course, that would explain it," Joym agreed. He nodded. "Most understandable."

"Indeed. Now, some of the young men there were more aggressive than others, and were not at all gentlemanly in their treatment of those around them."

"That's disgraceful," Joym said. "I must look into this."

Hesta looked at Godwyn. "We have a list of the names of the worst, should you wish it. My brother can provide details."

Joym nodded with great enthusiasm. "Indeed. Indeed."

Hesta took a deep breath. "Now, as you have probably noted, Evie here is exceptional at removing infections. She has a knack for it, and there is the patient from earlier who does not deserve to suffer for the behaviour of others. I think we should give him some assistance, don't you?"

"You are correct, Miss Bethwood. The man should not suffer because of the actions of others. Let me show you the way, and we'll see what we can do."

Hesta released a long sigh. "Yes, let's do that."

24

E vie stared at the pale man who lay unconscious in bed. She hadn't even touched him and her gift raged within her, bright, strong, and demanding that she use her powers.

"This is not right," she said. "This is very wrong."

"As wrong as I was when you first met me?" Hesta asked.

"Yes," Evie replied. "But different."

She pulled back the sheets to expose the man's abdomen and the surgical site where Ekvard had operated. There should have been a bleeding wound with poorly done stitches. What she found were burns where the skin had been fused together.

"Look familiar?" Evie asked.

Hesta raised her hand to her throat where her scarf covered her injuries. "The same?"

"No. Similar. I think they needed to do something extreme, otherwise he'd have died. Also it would be harder to hide a new set of stitches the size of this cut." Evie pressed against the scar. "What do you make of this, doctor?"

"It's an old burn," he answered.

"Not at all. This was the mark of surgery conducted but a few hours ago in your Rotunda."

"Impossible. This is weeks old," he responded.

"Can you help him?" Hesta asked.

"In all honesty, I don't know." Evie stared, and her gift gave her vision a wholly different perspective. Infections remained in the skin near the surgical site, but the searing heat used to melt the skin had killed much of the infection that she'd seen during the surgery. That was something.

What stood out most of all made her gift scream for attention. Worms. Little black crawling tendrils of an affliction that had no place on this earth. Some of them were longer and not so small either. A sac of something black circled around the man's throat, and slender lengths of this *thing* ran under his skull and searched through his brain.

Even if she could pull this creature out of his body, she wasn't entirely sure whether she could cure him.

She selected one of the little worms as it wriggled around the man's stomach. She put her hand on his belly and let her syphon gift pull at the blackness.

Crystals of ice formed on her eyelashes and burned at her eyelids. Her fingers turned purple and the ice crystals, so cold they burned, formed over her hands and crept up her arms.

She ground her teeth together as she pulled the worm from the man. She turned her hand over, and the blackness jerked about. Ice formed along the length of its body, and it disappeared in a burst of light.

"Damn," she said. "That was hard." She looked up, and Hesta drew a small piece of linen from her sleeve and wiped Evie's face.

"You're dripping something unpleasant from your eyes."

Evie looked at the corner of the cloth. It was covered with black and purple ooze. "Well, that doesn't happen often."

"How are you?" Hesta asked,

"This is very hard, but it needs to come out. I can't do much at once, though."

"What the hell is this?" Joym asked.

Evie turned to face him. "I am sorry, doctor, but this man has been infected with something hellish. And only I can…" Her words faded away. Out of the corner of her eye, she watched as a tendril of black reached from this patient and sought out the next bed.

"Can you see that?" Evie asked, and pointed.

"No," Hesta replied.

"I think it doesn't like being near me," Evie said, and she approached the escaping infection.

"What is it? What can you see?" Hesta said.

"No idea, but it's something. A beast, maybe, or an infection from another place."

"Hell?"

Evie shrugged. "I need to deal with this hell spawn before it infects everyone here." Her gift needed no encouragement. The threat increased with every second. It was easier now that this part of the spawn had extended out of Philip's body. She held her hands out, encouraged her gift, and pulled.

Black ice raced over her hands and arms. She could feel the cold forming over her face, too, and it tickled. How could ice tickle? But thoughts of the ice vanished as heat and cold collided within her chest and exploded in searing pain. She had it, this spawn, and it fought her. She didn't have enough strength for it.

Fibres of black laced around her fingers and looked for a way into her skin. She could see one wrapping around her arm as it wriggled in slimy certainty along her skin.

Evie screamed as she realised she didn't know how to deal with this *thing*.

'*I'm not enough!*' she screamed into Hesta's mind. '*It's trying to get into my head.*'

"No. Fight it, Evie," Hesta said.

"I'm trying. It's too much. I don't understand."

Hesta touched the back of Evie's neck with cool fingers. She wanted to lean back against those fingers and take comfort in a touch that had nothing to do with sickness and inflammation. But then Hesta sang to her. A gentle song that seemed to say, "You can do this. I have your back and my strength is yours."

It worked.

Evie's gift stepped up, took the song, and strengthened itself with the power of the siren.

She took a good grip of the writhing tentacle and a flash of searing heat burned through every part of her except her hands. Ice blossomed over her skin and grew so cold it almost froze her fingers. Black and purple crystals formed and spread to the black appendage in a wave of freezing ice.

"Go!" Evie screamed, and the ice shattered, taking the tentacle with it.

She almost collapsed, but Hesta caught her and helped her to stand.

"Are you all right?" Hesta asked.

Evie wiped her face and mouth on the back of her sleeve. Black oil and purple goo smeared across the fabric. "I'm a mess. I stink." She wobbled on her feet as she took a look at the man on the bed. "He's clean, apart from the remnants of normal infections. He should be fine."

Joym stood with his mouth open.

"You saw that?" Hesta asked.

He nodded.

"Doctor Montgomery, I think we all need tea and biscuits, or something to revive ourselves after that, don't you think?"

He nodded. "This way. We have a room where we might have a rest."

"And a place to wash up?" Evie asked.

"Yes, of course," he said. "I can get you spare clothing, too."

Evie looked down at herself. Black, purple, green, and yellow slimes, for want of a better description, covered her.

"Thank you. I appreciate that. I look and smell as though I've been in the sewers.

Hesta sniffed vaguely in Evie's direction. "You certainly do."

The doctor, good to his word, showed them into the room the doctors used for breaks and changes of clothing. A washing room was also available. The washing room had a large sink and a functional shower. Evie had seen one before, but it wasn't a regular part of most households. "A shower!"

Hesta joined Evie in the washing room. "Need a hand getting undressed?"

"You do know I'm more than capable of undressing."

Hesta turned a delicate shade of pink and looked away. "I didn't mean it like that."

"Of course not." Evie stood half undressed, made uncertain by Hesta's response. It wasn't that she considered herself the forward kind, but after years of life in captivity, she had become more than used to the lack of privacy that such a station in life engendered. Evie dropped her dirty clothing into the sink. She stood in her underthings for a moment as she considered how to phrase what she needed to say. Nothing diplomatic came to mind. She still had to say it, however.

"You know, you shouldn't touch me when I'm taking sickness into myself," she said.

"Why not? You needed help and the contact seemed to settle you, at least a little."

It did, but she wasn't prepared to admit as much. "No, it's just that when you make contact when I'm sponging—"

"Sponging. What a strange way to say it."

"Soaking up the infections, then. Anyway, when I'm doing that, there is a good chance I might purge into you, and that makes it far worse."

"You wouldn't do that," Hesta said, with such confidence it almost made Evie wince.

"Yes, I would. It's little more than a reflex, and that's why Godwyn wanted me to learn how to do it to order."

"Well, you didn't allow your instincts to take over. You're obviously in control of yourself and your gift."

"But I might not be every time."

"You won't slip, though." She sounded so sure and certain.

Evie couldn't argue with that certainty, no matter what she thought. "Not only that. You sang to me. I didn't know you could do that in such a way, and I wasn't immune."

"Nor did I, but I wanted to help so much, and when I touched you I knew how to do it."

"Interesting. It worked, so thank you. I'd not have beaten that thing without you. Now I think we need to learn more about your gift. What you can do, and how to do it."

"I think we need to know more about hell and its beasts first," Hesta said.

"You can write that down on the list of things we must do. After catching Ekvard. Our priority must be to stop the demon attached to him from infecting others."

"Oh yes, otherwise we'll have a plague all right. One that has no cure, except you," Hesta said.

"With your help." Evie smiled. "Let me clean up. This stink really is bad."

"Right." Hesta paused at the door. "I'll be with Godwyn and the doctor. I bet he has a lot of questions."

Evie's shower didn't take long. The water was not warm, but at least now her skin smelled of carbolic soap and not the goo and gloop of the *thing*. Whatever it was. A spare uniform had been placed next to the wash bowl, but it was not a good fit and probably belonged to a nurse who was at least six inches taller than Evie was. Even with a belt around her waist, the garment hung from her shoulders like an ill-fitting sack. Better material, of course, but over-sized nonetheless.

She joined the others in the staff break room. A cup of tea waited for her, and Hesta added honey to it as Evie came in.

"You need the energy," Hesta said by way of explanation.

Evie couldn't argue. She was grateful for anything she was given.

"Your clothes are ruined, you know," Hesta said.

"I needed new ones anyway, and I can afford them now that I have an income."

"Do you have more clothing at the Hickman house?"

Evie didn't really want to go into her personal business. Not with Hesta, and especially not with a man—two men—in the room.

For a moment, she couldn't understand her own hesitancy. She shook her head. "Some underthings and a couple of other pieces. But usually we wash, press, and wear them again."

Hesta looked at Godwyn. He sighed loudly and pointedly. "Understood. I'll try and arrange replacement clothing for the morning."

"Just like old times," Evie said.

He smirked at her. "The good ole days. Point taken, though. I know just the person to make such arrangements."

"And add additional clothing as well, Godwyn," Hesta added. "If tonight is anything to go by, then I think we'll need it."

"Consider it all in hand," he said.

Evie yawned. "I take it you've brought the doctor up to speed?"

"Yes," Hesta answered.

The doctor looked rather flustered. "I still find it hard to believe. Demons. A woman who can soak up infection and dispel the demons, too." He shook his head. "Inconceivable, really."

"I'd rather no one knew what I can do," Evie said.

"Quite. No one would believe me anyway."

"Let's leave it like that. But it seems to me that I need

more instruction on the body and infections and diseases so that I might be more effective," Evie said. "Yes, I need to know more. How would I do that?"

"You could be better?"

"Of course. I know that if I apply myself in the right way to certain sicknesses, the results are better. I always want to be better."

"Then you need to become a medic. Or a nurse."

"Nurse Chester," Evie said. "I like the sound of that."

"Or Medic Chester," Hesta said. "But you'll need to study."

She shrugged. "As soon as I learn to read."

Doctor Montgomery looked at her thoughtfully. "If you help me while you are studying, then I'll help you to learn about diseases."

Evie grinned. "That's a deal, sir. When can I start?"

"Tomorrow," he said.

Evie grinned even more.

25

By any standards, Bethwood House was a posh home. It had a proper kitchen, like all the big houses, with a large stove range, a walk-in pantry, and a huge table they could eat dinner at. Evie sat close to the stove and held out her hands to fend off the early morning chill.

A cup of tea sat on the table, and she'd helped herself to a thick slice of bread slathered in butter and thick raspberry jam. It tasted of ash in her mouth, and she didn't know why. Using her gift didn't usually kill her ability to taste. Of course, the one last night had been particularly vile. It would resolve itself. She hoped.

Maybe she just needed a little fresh air.

Evie opened the door into the back yard and stepped outside. It had rained overnight, and a mist clung to the buildings and the small walled garden to the back. She took a deep breath of cool morning air. And then froze. Outbuildings of various sizes stood along the west wall of the garden. There were several wooden sheds, too, like the pens she had lived in.

Fear gripped her chest with icy claws until she could barely breathe.

"No."

She staggered to the first of the outbuildings, a small pig-pen with a chest-high wall surrounding the feed bowl and a small pigsty to protect the animal from the worst of the weather. She saw no pig, though. There was no lock on the gate, so she went inside the enclosure. It was empty of everything except a little debris from the collapsed roof. Evie leaned against the damp wall and took a few deep breaths to settle her thudding heart.

It wasn't enough to check one building. She needed to be sure, so she raced from shed to shed. Although not a single outbuilding had a functioning lock, she had to look inside, to be absolutely certain. None of them were inhabited. And by the state of the interiors, they had never been used for anything other than the storage of animal feed, pots, and tools for the garden.

The stable contained two black horses, and they stared at her as she entered. This stable wasn't like the one she'd been forced to live in, but she still searched for the additions that Florie had created to provide them with water. Just in case.

Once she had been satisfied that this wasn't the same place, she leaned against the corner of the block and slumped down to the floor. She sat on cold stone, her back protected by the brick wall. Evie covered her face and huddled into a ball where she sat.

Her terror had been real and had almost overwhelmed her. All this time, playing at being free, and it could all be taken away so easily. The door to the stables opened, and someone came inside. Evie didn't look. A part of her expected to be cast in chains right then and there. Could the fear of a lifetime of enforced bondage be undone so fast? She wiped away her tears. No. Fear and memories did not go away just like that. She would never forget.

Still, she couldn't quite muster the strength to face anyone.

Someone knelt down in front of her. She knew that it was Hesta without looking.

"Evie." She moved Evie's hands so they no longer hid her face. "It's all right," she said, and stroked Evie's cheek with the back of her hand.

Evie looked up and stared at Hesta.

"It'll be fine," she said, and wrapped her arms around Evie. That was all she said. There was nothing more that could be said.

Evie cried outright then, and her whole body shook with sobs she'd not known she had. All the way through, Hesta held her close and stroked her back. Evie liked the contact—needed it, even.

When the tears stopped, Hesta didn't move. Evie didn't want this moment of comfort to end. Nor did she want to let Hesta see quite how distraught she felt. She would know, she had held her whilst she'd sobbed her heart out, but she could hide it so long as Hesta didn't see her face. She looked up eventually, uncertain what reaction she might find.

Hesta pushed Evie's hair from her face and wiped her tears away with a square white cotton handkerchief. She didn't say anything, even now, but helped Evie to stand up.

"I…" Evie started.

Hesta touched Evie's lips with her finger to say that words were not needed. Then she wrapped Evie in her arms and held her tight. For a moment, Evie felt her tears well up again. She leaned into Hesta, took comfort in her presence, and let uncertainty fall away.

"I'm all right," Evie said, her voice weak and thin.

"Shhh." Hesta held her tighter, and Evie tucked her head against Hesta's neck. When being close to another person no longer felt strange or odd, she put her arms around her waist and held on tight. It was such an unusual thing for her to do. But she liked it, and Evie didn't want it to stop. After all, it might never happen again.

Hesta moved first. She leaned back until the space grew between them. "How are you doing?"

"Better," Evie managed. "I saw the buildings, and…and for a moment, I thought it was the place I had been kept."

"I understand."

"Do you? How could you? Now I need to look at every room in the house. I have to make certain."

Hesta nodded, took her by the hand, and led her back into the house.

Evie stopped just before the back door. But she'd been inside already, and there were no threats outside. One deep breath, and Evie found the strength to go inside again.

They went from room to room. Ground floor, first floor, and the second storey. She saw a makeshift bed in one of the smallest rooms under the eaves.

"Godwyn stays here," Hesta said.

"Where is he?"

"He left early, I think. He usually does. It's his way. He thinks life will pass him by if he sleeps long or with too much comfort."

Evie absorbed that information and filed it in her mind with all the other bits of information she'd acquired about the Bethwoods. Just in case. It seemed she wasn't the only one who had demons of one sort or another.

"There is only one area left to see." Hesta took Evie's hand and led her back down the stairs, almost to the library.

Under the stairs, and out of plain sight, Evie saw another doorway.

"Basement," Hesta said. "Let me show you." Just through the doorway, she flicked a switch and light flooded a rough set of steps down.

"You don't have electrics all around the house?"

"Not yet. I will, but it is not a cheap thing to do, and it seems a luxury," Hesta answered. "Come on."

They clattered down the stairs into an underground area

not quite the size of the house. The walls were very thick and separated the whole area into sections. A chute in one corner with sacks of coal and logs sat next to a furnace.

"When we are fully established, we'll have someone to make sure we have heat all day and night."

"Not slaves!" Evie said with some force.

Hesta shook her head. "Not at all. I was hoping to take on a couple of people to help take care of us. Waged, of course, with their own rooms and benefits."

"Like food and warmth."

"Of course, as well as subsidized clothing and medical care."

Evie nodded. "Good." She slipped her arm through Hesta's. "So, what are we up to today? We have a demon surgeon to find."

"Yes, we do. So I thought today we could have a short reading lesson, then we could go and see Mrs. Hickman so she doesn't fret. Then we'll go and visit Galeazzi Poul at the hall of the vitalists." She flushed a shade of pink. "Then I thought I would take you somewhere nice for dinner, just you and me. If you would like that." Hesta looked away, as though she didn't want to expose herself to the possibility of a rejection.

"That sounds lovely," Evie said. "Should we wait for Godwyn?"

"Do you want Godwyn with us?"

Evie shook her head vigorously. "I find his presence disturbing," she admitted.

"Then it'll be just us. And I'm glad, because I'd like you all to myself without you worrying about my brother. Or anyone else."

"There's no one else for me to worry about except Agatha and Florie."

"And me," Hesta said. "Don't forget me."

"I hardly know you."

"Doesn't matter. Looking after you is one of my responsibilities, and I take such things very seriously."

"I am not *your* responsibility, Hesta Bethwood. That sounds too much like ownership, and that will never happen again."

26

E vie stood outside the house with Hesta as Charlie and his calash pulled up to the curb.

"Morning, Charlie," Evie said.

He raised his cap. "Morning, Miss Chester, Miss Bethwood."

"We're going to see the vitalists at the hall opposite Stake Island," Evie said.

"I know it," he said.

"Good. First, I need to make a little detour," Hesta said.

"Wherever you want to go, it would be my pleasure. I am all yours for as long as you need me."

"And we're not in any rush," Hesta said. "Do you know all of the houses owned by my brother?"

Charlie scratched the side of his face. "All? I'm not so sure about every house, but I know five of them. There are two in the Badesville district, one in Cainstown, close to Ardmore, one in Blest Hill, and one near Queens park."

"That sounds about right," Hesta said.

"Where to first?" he asked.

"If you drive around the Queens Park address first, we'll

probably not have to stop, but I might change my mind. Then to Badesville, followed by Blest Hill, and then Cainstown."

"A circular tour it is," Charlie said. "Settle in and we'll be off."

Evie sat down and pulled a travel rug over her knees. "Why are we looking at your brother's houses?"

Hesta reached over to touch Evie's hand. "I want you to see if any of them look familiar, and you must tell me what you recall of these places."

"Why?"

"I'm going to make sure these places are never used to house slaves ever again."

"You said he wasn't doing that kind of thing anymore."

"Yes, and I believe him. But I need you to be certain and believe in him, too. If any of them hold memories, then this is the time to face them and do as you see fit. It might bring you some peace."

Evie stared forward at their driver's back. She took a moment to think things through. "All right. Let's do that."

The first house, at the end of the crescent, had no outbuildings to speak of, nor did it look familiar. "I don't know this one," she said.

"I didn't think you would. This is his main house."

"No point looking any closer, then."

"Charlie, on to Badesville," Hesta said.

Evie didn't think she had ever been to Badesville. None of the streets looked familiar, although she thought one of the main roads looked familiar enough that it might have been one of those she'd travelled along. Maybe it led to one of the posh houses that Godwyn had taken her to.

They stopped outside a house in Badesville. It didn't look very familiar to her either. Mostly because it looked too small and compact. Her heart, which had pounded all the way through Badesville, started to settle. This wasn't the place. But they stopped to look nonetheless. Hesta knocked at the door, and an old chap, stooped and bent with age, opened the door.

"Hello, I am Hesta Bethwood."

"Rent ain't due yet, "he said.

"Of course not, that is for you and my brother to discuss. I'm trying to find the house where my good friend stayed until a little while ago."

"The others are more recent, but I've been here five years and she don't look at all familiar," he said.

"That's all I needed to know. Thank you for your time."

The same was true of the other Badesville residence. Although the second one had a small outbuilding, it contained nothing more than coal and wood for the stove.

Evie's heart didn't slow down again until they turned back to the eastern end of Bristelle and towards Blest Hill to the south of the airfield for cargo airships. Now this area seemed familiar, and her breath caught in her throat as she recognised some of the landmarks. A hardware store at the corner of a street, and a roundabout with a bush in the middle that represented a very unusual road feature in the city.

Her hand found Hesta's, and she gripped so hard she lost sensation in her fingers.

"Evie?" Hesta asked.

"I know this place," she said.

"Are you all right with this? We can stop."

Evie shook her head vehemently. "No. Let me do this."

They stopped on the street outside a reasonably large and detached residence surrounded by a wall and topped with iron railings. It didn't mean much to her.

"Go round the back," she said, her voice low, little more than a breathy whisper. "I need to see the back."

Charlie drove around the corner to the alley that would give access to the rear gate. She recognised the gates, and they were open.

"I think this is it."

"We won't move until you're sure."

Evie's eyes darted to the back of the house and then to the range of outbuildings further back. She didn't need to recognise any of them, however, when a man she knew swaggered towards the calash. Grobber.

She stiffened in her seat, and as he drew closer, she tried to push herself so far into the carriage that he wouldn't see her. But this was a calash; there weren't many places to hide.

"Good day," Grobber said as he approached. He stopped when he recognised at least one of the women inside.

"Miss Bethwood, what brings you here? Your brother isn't here," he said.

"I'm not here for Godwyn. I'm here to have a look around the house."

"But—"

"No buts, thank you. You are?"

"Grobber," Evie whispered. "That's Grobber."

"Mr. Grobber," he said.

"I see. You're Grobber." She made a show of staring at him. "Indeed, I understand the resemblance."

"Miss Bethwood?"

Hesta opened the door and stepped out of the calash. "We want to look through the gardens and outbuildings first, Mr. Grobber."

"But I would need to ask Mr. Bethwood if—"

"He would never deny me, Mr. Grobber. I suggest you don't either." She turned to Evie. "Come on, Evie, let's take a look around."

Evie tried to push herself further into the seating. "I already know this place."

"And we will know it better yet," Hesta said.

"Is that the girl?" Grobber asked.

"It is," Hesta said. She held out her hand. "Come on, Evie. Nothing and no one will hurt you. You have my word."

Evie didn't move.

"Deep breath, Evie. Take a deep breath and face this man and this place," she whispered.

Evie took a breath, and her attention remained on Hesta's face. Hesta took a deep breath with her, and Evie could feel at least a little courage return to her limbs.

"Yes. Let's look at the outbuildings."

"This is hard, I know, and I am proud of you for facing this."

Grobber glared at Evie when she stepped out of the carriage. "Is there a problem?" she asked.

"What the fuck are you doing here?"

"Mind your language," Hesta said.

"Pardon me miss Bethwood," he replied.

Evie took one final deep breath and brought her shoulders back. She answered him with as much confidence as she could muster. "Grobber, I have every right to be wherever the hell I choose. I choose to be here."

She turned away from him and headed towards the stables first. She closed her eyes when she opened the unlocked door.

She held her breath and opened her eyes. The space was empty.

Still, the evidence that they had been here remained, including a half full slop bucket and a damp and dirty blanket. The pipework that Florie had rigged together to provide them with water was still intact. If she were to reach into the rafters, would she find the food she and Florie had hidden for when meals were in short supply?

She pointed into the far corner. "That's where we slept, Florie and I." Then she pointed near the door. "And that is where they dumped me when they thought I was dying."

Hesta looked horrified, and Evie took some perverse pleasure in the fact that she could make a Bethwood feel uncomfortable.

"Come," Evie said, and led the way to one of the sheds. There were no slaves inside, but their shackles and the bars of their cages remained. "This is where they put everyone whose gifts and behaviour were uncertain." She closed her eyes. "I started in here, and we would be given food only twice a week until we were broken enough to do as we were told."

"Oh, Evie, I am so sorry."

Evie didn't wait to listen. She marched from shed to shed to make certain they were all empty. When she was sure, she made her way into the house. She found the room, the one with the windows boarded over, the chair in the corner, and the bed next to the wall with the manacles still attached.

"This is where they chained me." She stood in the middle of the room. "And this is where Eric died. They made me heal him, and then they…No, not *they*… Your brother made me kill him with my gift."

Hesta reached out to Evie, but she stepped away from her. "No. Don't touch me. I killed a man right here in this room, and still your brother was not happy. He didn't want me to heal you, he wanted me as an assassin."

Evie took one last look at the room. "I'm done here. I'd like to burn it all down, but that might be a little extreme."

Hesta smiled, but it looked tentative at best.

"Let's go," Evie said. "I never want to see this house again."

"Done." Hesta said.

Evie waited until they were back in the calash. Her back hurt from keeping it so straight and still. "Thank you."

"I didn't do anything."

"You helped me to face this horror."

"I wish I could make it go away."

"It was a start. I walked in, and I walked out because I chose to. It's a very good start."

"Do you want to see the other house?"

Evie shook her head. "This is enough for one day. But if I brought Florie, she would make sure it burned to the ground, no matter what I might say."

27

Evie let her thoughts wander as Charlie drove them into Cainstown. Hesta didn't bother her with pointless comments and seemed to recognise Evie's need for quiet.

They stopped outside the hall of the vitalists, and when she saw Stake Island, it sent shivers down her spine. The walls looked darker, blacker, and the buildings had grown taller and more imposing. Even the few people walking the nearby streets seemed to hunch over whenever they approached sight of the island. As though, if they made themselves small enough, the darkness of the prisons wouldn't notice they were there. A kind of "there but for the grace of the Mother of us all go I."

"You're never going there again," Hesta said, as though she'd read Evie's mind.

"I hope not. I would rather die than go to that island again."

"Don't look at it," Hesta said.

"How can I avoid it, though, when it stands on the river and you can't miss any of it no matter where you stand?"

Once again, Hesta grew quiet, as though she knew that Evie needed to find her own way out of the darkness. Evie was grateful for that slight change in approach. Hesta couldn't fix her or make her feel better about the world. But just being there, without interference, seemed to make a difference.

Evie took a deep breath. "I'm ready. Shall we go inside?"

"Charlie," Hesta said to the driver. "We'll probably be about an hour, if that. If you need to go elsewhere that's fine."

"Thank you, miss, but I'll wait for you right here," he replied.

"If we are not out in an hour, go get her brother," Evie said.

Hesta stared at her.

"Well, best be safe and take precautions, just in case."

"Got that," Charlie said. "If there is a problem, I know where to find him."

"Good man," Hesta said. She got out of the carriage and held out her arm. "Shall we go in now, Evie?"

Inside the reception room, the view was much like it had been before, but now there were few people around. A woman sat next to the reception table, and a couple of minders stood next to her in the immortal pose of the thug on a job, legs splayed and hands held together in front of the body.

"Yes?" asked the woman.

"Is Galeazzi here?" Hesta asked.

"He's busy," she said.

"He's not too busy for us," Hesta said.

The two men approached them. "Problem?" asked one.

"These women were just leaving," the woman said.

Hesta looked at Evie. "I don't think they understand what I'm saying."

"Maybe you should make it clearer. I know you could be more persuasive if you put some effort into it," Evie suggested.

"Are you sure this is all right to do?"

Evie nodded.

"Excuse me," one of the men said, the same one who had spoken before. "I think it is time for you to leave."

Hesta didn't sing as such, but as she spoke, Evie could feel the touch of the siren as the magic brushed over her ears. "Don't you recognise me? I'm from the theater, and not only is Galeazzi expecting us, he is looking forward to us being here. He will be happy, so very happy when we see him. And happy and pleased that you were the ones who bought us to him. Is he here? If he is out, you can tell us where he is."

The woman looked up, her eyes not so much glazed as adoring.

"Do you want to tell him that Hesta and Evie are here?" Hesta asked with the slightest brush of her magic.

The woman didn't look away as she spoke to one of the thugs. "Jon, take them to his rooms, will you? He'll be so pleased to see them here."

Jon led them up the stairs to a long hallway with doors on either side. Their footsteps echoed against the wooden floorboards as they strode the full length of the hall to the door at the end. Jon knocked and waited a moment. At the sound of someone moving about on the other side, Jon said, "Mr. Poul, there are two ladies for you."

The door opened, and Galeazzi stared out. "What?" Then he saw who it was. "Miss Bethwood. Miss Chester. Thank you, Jon. Much appreciated."

"Right," Jon said, and he left them there.

"Please, come in. Excuse me for the lack of comforts in my rooms."

As they walked inside, Evie saw that lack of comfort was an understatement. A table with two chairs, a washstand with a bowl and jug, and, in the corner, a small narrow bed with a pull-out mattress underneath.

"How is your son?" Hesta asked.

"He is well, thank you." He gestured to the chairs. "Please sit, if you wish."

"I'm happy to stand," Evie said.

"Can I get you tea? We have facilities downstairs, if you would like some."

"No, thank you," Hesta said.

"To what do I owe the pleasure?" he asked

"Ekvard," Evie said. "Where is he, and what do you know about him?"

"What? Why?"

Something in the corner of the room caught Evie's eye. She recognised the little thing straight away, and the power of it pulsed at her gift like a distress beacon. Would it know if she looked at it?

She turned her head a little, and the worm thing stretched itself out until it became no more than a thread of itself. It pulsed with an eerie eldritch light and then faded in and out of her gift sight. It was a most difficult creature to observe, and without her gift she wouldn't see it at all.

She focussed her gaze on Galeazzi, and he seemed uneasy under her intense scrutiny. He had not been touched. Yet. But he would be soon, she was sure of that.

"What are you doing?" he asked,

"Where is your son?" Evie demanded

"What?" he asked.

"Where is your boy?"

"He's with his tutor. I couldn't get him into the school, and they bully him when I do, so I get him a private master."

Evie nodded. "Very well. I need to see him when he is done."

"Why?"

"Because everything you do and everything you touch has been infected."

"Bless me, Father," he said.

"Oh, he's no use here," Evie assured him. "Neither is the

Mother, or any other Gods you might create or know of. They are powerless." She shrugged and turned her attention to the bed.

"Are these cot things comfortable?" she asked.

"They are acceptable," he said, and joined her next to the bed.

"Strong and solid?" she asked.

"I suppose…"

"Good." Evie hoisted her skirts to her knees and jumped onto the bed. Her gift flared as she drew closer to the fading thread of the creature. She held out both hands to grab it, and the freezing chill of the beyond rushed out of her fingers and covered the creature. Now it could be seen, and no matter how much it tried to struggle away, Evie had it.

Hesta jumped up beside her, and warm fingers touched the back of her neck. "You have this. Send that monster back," she said. Again, Evie could feel the tingle of her words brush against her ears. And then the thread shattered, and purple-tinted ice covered the bed and the floor.

Hesta grinned. "I think you should tell my brother we both jumped in the same bed."

Evie snorted. "Hesta Bethwood, you have a singular kind of humour."

"Yes, and now your cheeks are pink and warm, not covered in cold and ice. I think that's a win, don't you?"

"What the hell was that?" Galeazzi asked, before Evie could reply.

Evie rolled her shoulders and turned her attention to him. "Nothing much. Just a demon spawn come to take over your mind and body."

"A *what*?"

Hesta jumped off the bed but spared a glance towards Evie. " I think your humour is as dark as mine."

"Yes," Evie agreed. "And these damned skirts are a nuisance for days like this."

173

"Please, will you tell me what is going on? And then tell me why you asked about my son?"

Evie took a deep breath. "There is no point talking all nice and sweet, so we must make this quite plain. Ekvard is host to a major demon, and he is trying to infect people with it. He has already done so with the man he used for his demonstration."

"That thing we just killed was one of them," Hesta added.

"You can't be right. The very idea of such things as demons and so on sounds insane."

"Insane?" Evie asked. "What about the attack that almost killed your son outside? Is it normal to find so many people writhing on the ground in agony with such swelling of the brain that it almost kills them?"

"Well, no," he admitted.

"I think we'll have to test the whole building and everyone in it, don't you?" Evie asked.

Hesta nodded. "I agree."

"We should have this place locked down until everything is cleared. No one in or out until they've been tested and we've searched the rooms."

"You can't do that," Galeazzi said. "What would we say to them?"

"I suggest you use your powers of persuasion and the animal magnetism you go on about," Hesta said. "Get them to attend a free performance. You must get them together."

Galeazzi didn't look convinced.

"Trust me," Evie said. "You have no idea how bad this could get."

"Do you?" he asked.

"I've seen what the main demon can do, and I've seen what the little ones are capable of as well. You don't want them running riot around the whole city."

28

E vie stood at the window and looked outside. Across the way she could see Stake Island, but somehow being on the second floor made the prison island appear less formidable. "How many floors are there in this building, and what are they used for?"

"The ground floor is mostly reception and some rooms that they use for offices and such things. The first floor is for the meeting and demonstration rooms along with a place that serves drinks," Galeazzi said. "Second floor, this one, is accommodation rooms. Not all of them are used at the moment. Upstairs, the top floor, is for storage only. No one is there."

Hesta looked at Evie. "I think that would be a great place to put things you didn't want others to find."

"I agree. So, Galeazzi, get as many people as you can into the meeting room. Lock and secure all doors into the building. No one leaves or enters until we're sure it's clean..."

"Clean of disease," Hesta finished.

"Perfect." She turned to Galeazzi. "Can you do that?"

He swallowed hard and then nodded. "Yes. Will you come with me?"

"No." Evie answered. 'We'll check the rooms on this floor and then come downstairs to the meeting room."

"Then the ground floor," Hesta suggested.

"Yes. Ground floor." Evie rubbed her hands together at the thought of what they might find. "Now, move quickly. The sooner we get this done, the sooner the building will be safe."

Galeazzi raced outside, and they followed him out at a slower pace. He banged on the doors as he rushed by and yelled out, "New tests and processes in the meeting room. Free healing to all. Come now, before it's too busy." He repeated the message over and over and knocked on every door.

Doors opened along the corridor. People stepped out to see what the fuss was about. "What's going on?"

"New healing," Hesta said. "The mesmerist has had an idea about how to make his skills better and work faster. He can take away all of your aches and pains."

Many of the people who'd opened their door to Galeazzi followed him down the stairs at the far end of the hallway.

Evie knocked on the first door to her right, and when no one answered, she tried the handle. It was unlocked. She stared into the first room, but her gift found nothing of consequence. "Nothing," she said.

She closed the door and knocked on the door opposite.

One by one, Evie and Hesta opened the doors along the corridor. None were locked. In fact, many of the doors were not even lockable.

"It's not very secure, is it?" Hesta observed.

"It's not really a place to turn into a home."

"It's more of a temporary stay, then?"

Evie nodded. "There's nothing homey here. It's a place to stay for the sort of people who have to move wherever the work is."

Hesta knocked on the last door but didn't wait to open it.

"Oi!" shouted an unhappy voice. A man wearing a pair of

work trousers and a vest stood, hands on hips, in the middle of the room.

Evie stepped inside and glanced around. "Sorry," she said. "You do know there is a free demonstration downstairs?"

"Piss off. It's all a con," he said. "That Ekvard claimed he could cure my backache earlier, but he can't."

"I'm sorry about that," Hesta said. "Was that today?"

"Yeah, a couple of hours ago. Left me with a throbbing head instead of making me better," he said.

"Let me look," Evie said.

"Not if you are one of them. No point, is there?"

"She's different, I promise," Hesta said.

Evie let her gift rise as she moved behind the man. She could see some soreness in the muscles and the joints, but it was too general and diffuse. It didn't look like anything she could help with. "I'm not sure I can help here. The damage is all along your back. Do you do any heavy lifting?"

"I do."

Evie placed her hands on his back, and she pulled and teased at the inflamed areas. It wasn't much, but his back responded to that small measure of healing.

"Well, I never," he said.

"I can't cure you. I think you need to be more careful about how you lift things. Don't force your back to take the strain."

He stretched and twisted. "Almost good as new. Thank you."

"It's not as good as new. You must take more care when you work."

"Back straight, knees bent," Hesta suggested.

"Exactly that. Protect your back, or you'll wear it out," Evie said. "Or look for a job with less lifting. You're welcome."

"Do you know where Ekvard's room is?" Hesta asked.

He shrugged. "Never seen him in one. He likes to check

on his storage boxes upstairs, but he ain't here right now. He went out."

"Thanks," Evie said as they left. The door closed behind them with a *thud*. Her thoughts slowed her step.

"What's up?" Hesta asked.

"Just putting it all together."

At the stairwell, Hesta stopped. "Should we go upstairs, then, if Ekvard uses it a lot?"

"Not now. He's out anyway, so we have plenty of time for that. Right now, I'm more worried people will leave the building before we can check them."

"Especially if they are contaminated?"

"Exactly."

Evie started down the stairs now that she had a plan in mind. "Let's go to the ground floor, make sure it is all shut tight, and then we'll check the people in the meeting room."

At the front doors, the two minders stood next to the entrance door in their obligatory threatening pose.

"Sorry, you can't go out right now," the woman at the reception desk said.

"I know, thank you for your diligence," Hesta said.

"We just need to check the other rooms on this floor for Galeazzi."

"The back doors are locked," said one of the men.

"What are your names?" Hesta asked.

The one who'd spoken pointed at himself. "I'm Dadge, and this is Harry."

Evie scanned the room, but she saw no sign of anything untoward.

"Let me just look in all the rooms just in case," Evie said. "We must be very sure."

The two men looked at each other.

"Come on, Dadge," Hesta said, infusing her voice with a bit of her gift. "Show us everything."

"Mind the door," he said, and then showed the two

women all around the ground floor. Some of the rooms had locks, but Dadge had the key. Nothing was beyond their access. But in the end, there was nothing for them to see.

"We're all clear here. Just keep it locked up until we get back," Hesta said. "We'll go to the meeting, and then check the top floor."

"You can't get up there," Dadge said. "There are new locks and things, and this is the old key not the new one."

"Who has the key?" Evie asked.

"Ekvard has the only set," he answered.

"And where is Ekvard?"

"He's gone out to some kind of meeting with a fancy investor at some fancy named house," he said. "Bethwood House, I think. Wherever that is."

Hesta froze. "Ekvard has gone to see Godwyn Bethwood?"

"That's the chap," Harry said. "Meeting at Bethwood House."

Evie rushed to Hesta's side and helped support her. She looked far too disturbed by the news.

"It will be all right, Hesta. Let me just check the meeting room, and then we'll go."

Hesta nodded.

"Sooner started…" Evie said.

"Sooner finished," Hesta finished.

29

I t took some time to clear the meeting hall, and when they got outside, Charlie and the calash could not be seen. Evie stared up and down the street, but this was not the most popular thoroughfare, and there were no cabs anywhere.

"Damn," Hesta said.

"Never mind, this way. We'll find a carriage the moment we get closer to a main road."

They rushed through the busy streets of Cainstown, gathering looks as they dashed in a most unfeminine fashion down the narrow streets. They were almost all the way to Ardmore Street when a familiar calash and driver came clattering in their direction. Charlie drew to a stop, his horse all lathered and chomping at the bit. "Miss Bethwood," he said. "I was most worried when you were rather longer than the hour you said. I tried the door and it was locked."

Hesta clambered into the carriage with Evie behind her. "I know. I'm sorry."

"I went to find Mr Bethwood, but he's not at his house. No one knows where he is," Charlie said.

"That's all right. Take us to Bethwood House straight

away. We should find him there. Well, I hope we do," Hesta said.

"I'm sorry if I let you down," he said.

"No, Charlie. It's a day of strange and unpredictable events," Evie said. "And I know you have been rushing about, but any speed you can manage would be helpful. I think Mr Bethwood is in need of assistance."

"Right away, ma'am." He clicked his tongue and shook the reins a little, and the horse moved on. He had to drive farther into Cainstown before the road widened enough that he could turn around. Then he clattered along the roads as fast as the other road users could allow.

It felt like hours to get to Bethwood house. Hesta sat on the edge of the seat all the way and looked terrified. The moment they arrived, she almost launched herself from the carriage before it had come to a rest.

Evie followed with alacrity. No matter what she thought of Godwyn Bethwood, he was Hesta's brother. If he was in trouble, then they had to save him.

"Do you need me?" Charlie called out.

"We'll be fine, thank you, Charlie," Evie said. "I think we're done for the day."

He raised his cap. "Good day to you both."

On the porch, Hesta fumbled for her keys, but Evie put her hand over hers and took them away. "Let me," she said. It took two tries before she found the right one, but as soon as she turned the key, the door swung open into a dark and silent hallway.

"Godwyn!" Hesta called out.

"Come through to the drawing room. I'm here," he answered.

Hesta started to rush for the door, but Evie grabbed her arm and slowed her down. "Calm yourself. I need you to be steady. We might have nothing to—"

"Yes, of course," Hesta replied, but she pulled away and raced into the drawing room.

Evie followed with a little more caution, and as soon as she stepped into the room, her gift sprang to life. It was hard not to respond to the overwhelming shriek of "wrong," and that sense almost overwhelmed the details.

Godwyn stood with his hands forward as though to fend off Hesta. At his side stood Ekvard, his facial features slack and unexpressive.

"Stop!" Evie shouted. She reached out and gripped Hesta's arm with one hand; her other snagged the material of Hesta's skirt.

"Let me go," Hesta said.

Evie gripped her even harder, hard enough to leave bruises on Hesta's arm. Hard enough to fear the chance of ripping her clothing, too. Under no circumstances would she let Hesta get any closer.

"No. Stop and think." In the moment that Hesta paused, Evie dashed in front of her so she could stand between her and the two men. She would be a shield for the moment.

"What?" Hesta asked, and stopped still. "Godwyn?"

"Hesta, you should not have come," Godwyn said. His face was contorted in pain.

"Actually, I for one am glad that you are here," Ekvard said. "It is the whole reason why we are here at all."

"Ekvard and friend," Evie said. The dark life that had attached to him pulsed with unnatural energy. Tendrils of black wafted above his head and tethered him to Godwyn. "And now you have infected Godwyn with your foulness."

"What?" Hesta asked.

"The thing on Ekvard has infected Godwyn," Evie said. "Plain as day."

The creature attached to Edvard stiffened, and it's body elongated as though to stare over his shoulder at Evie. A heartbeat later, Ekvard also turned to stare at Evie. "You can see us?"

"Yes, I can see you," Evie said, "and I know what you can do. I don't know why, though"

The bulbous creature lifted itself up and stretched out, as though trying to sniff at Evie. "What are you?" Ekvard asked.

"No one," Evie replied.

"Not who. *What* are you?" he asked again.

"Just someone who wants to help," Evie answered. "You said you were here for someone?"

"Sirens are mine," he said.

"Ahh, I see," Evie said. "You like singers. Were the sonos attacks from you, or someone else?"

"Sirens are mine."

"Looks like you have a persistent admirer," Evie said. She focused on Godwyn. "What about you, Godwyn? Are you there, or is the puppet master in control of you as well?"

Ekvard hissed like a snake. "I am no puppet master."

"Good as," she said.

Godwyn grimaced and shook his head.

"Not totally in control, then," Evie observed.

"Three times we have sought the siren, wanting her to rejoin us, and three times she has refused. The last time she bore the curse of her refusal. Now, our requests are more determined."

"If you want her, then why infect another?"

"Hosting our progeny is an honor," it said through Ekvard's mouth. "The opportunity for growth arose, and we did not refuse."

Hesta stepped closer to Evie and rested her hands on her shoulders. "I don't understand. Why me?"

Evie watched as the body swung from side to side and the tentacles grew longer and thicker around Ekvard. Coldness settled inside her gut, and ice crept through her veins. With every passing second, she grew more ready for the fight she knew would come.

'Hesta, this is going to be a big fight. I will need your strength,' she said to Hesta's mind.

'I thought you did not like people speaking inside your mind?'

'Needs must. And I need everything if we are to save your brother.'

'Whatever you need,' Hesta replied.

"She asked you a question, thingie. Why her?" Evie demanded aloud.

"She is hell's daughter, and the Asirvi-Ars of the Egin'Ars demands it," he replied.

"The who arse of the what arse?"

"The king of the Over-Throne requires her services. She has refused the prince and his daughter, so now the king is free to make his own demands."

"Why now?" Hesta asked.

Ekvard pointed to his neck. "Those that can sense such things noted that your mark of the underworld had started to fade, and so we had to return before you were lost to us."

"Without those scars, you cannot find her?" Evie asked.

"We will always find those we seek," he replied.

"How did you get here? Is it possible for me to go to hell?" Evie asked.

'Evie!' Hesta said, straight into her mind.

"I'm curious," Evie said aloud.

"You open a portal between the realms and step through," Ekvard said.

"So you are here to grab her and step through such a portal?" Evie asked. "Could I open one?"

Ekvard laughed. "Death is the portal. She dies, I die, and we return to our place."

"You both die?"

"And are resurrected under the eternal life of the king of the realm, the Over-Throne."

Hesta shivered and pressed herself against Evie's back.

"Is there room for negotiation?" Evie asked.

Ekvard stared at her. "Negotiation? A stupid question. You do not negotiate with the Underworld."

"Maybe you should start," Evie suggested. "Maybe it would make the whole process a little less fraught for all concerned."

'Evie, what are you doing?' Hesta almost screeched inside Evie's mind.

'I'm trying to make him angry,' Evie responded.

"It's working," Hesta observed dryly. She sounded confident, but Evie could feel the tremble in her hands.

Evie never took her eyes off the beast or any of its tendrils. Godwyn didn't move, and neither did Ekvard. Just as Evie had noticed during the demonstration, the beast could only control so much.

"Did you know you were a hell spawn, Hesta?" Evie asked over her shoulder.

"No."

"Ahh, well now. It looks like I learn more about you each and every passing day."

"Stop being funny," Hesta said.

"Hey, what if I say no, you can't have her?" Evie asked.

Ekvard jerked as though she'd taken him by surprise. "No?"

"Yeah. You're a slimy half octopus or jellyfish thing that isn't really real, has no power, and can't really give me an answer of any worth. I think you're just a stupid messenger boy. An ugly one at that."

"Evie!" Hesta cried out.

"I'll show you. It's easy enough to take you as well as the siren and these bodies," Ekvard said, pointing to himself and Godwyn.

"Well, I don't think you can," she said. She took a step closer to Ekvard. *'I will need your help, Hesta.'*

'Always.'

Evie took another step forward, and as the space between her and the demon shrank, the gift within her grew stronger and more powerful. The chill that rolled like a wave through her body left her shivering. She clenched her hands into fists to stop herself from shaking, and ice crunched beneath her fingers.

Ekvard, or the creature controlling him, looked momentarily confused.

"I knew I'd scare you," Evie goaded. "I think you are all scary talk and no action. You can't control two bodies at the same time, so I wonder if I should just get a blade and slice you in two?"

"Fool!" Ekvard shouted. Black tentacles grew thick and solidified, others twirled in the air in tendrils so thin they looked like puffs of mist.

"Am I?" she asked, and took another step forward. Ekvard matched her step, and now the distance between them could be measured in just a couple of feet. The smell of something unpleasant filled the air. Like an open sewer, only worse. Under this, a distinct mustiness tickled her nose, and she almost sneezed.

The moment her attention wavered, Ekvard, with the creature and all the waving tendrils, dashed forward. Thick and heavy tentacles wrapped around her. But the moment that any part of it made contact with her skin, her gift exploded in a burst of freezing cold. The creature stopped, almost as though it had been frozen by her gift. It shivered and resumed pulling her closer.

"Now!" Evie yelled. Before the tentacles pinned her down, she stretched her hands out towards the heart of the beast.

Her vision blurred, and the colours of the room faded to shades of black and purple. Her power took the beast by surprise. Even more surprise followed when Hesta's gift joined hers, strengthened her, filled her with the joy of her own invincibility.

"No!" the beast cried out with Ekvard's voice.

Cold, the freezing cold of the place beyond all life, filled her and flowed into and through the beast. It screamed. Ekvard backhanded her with a force that no human could possess, yet she remained encased in the black coils of the beast. Then Godwyn, his eyes black and empty, wrapped his large, meaty hands around her throat. He squeezed until Evie struggled to breathe.

"Godwyn, no!" Hesta said, her voice all sing-song and yet commanding at the same time. The touch of her gift brushed against Evie's ears. The strength she gave to Evie vanished, and her command flowed instead through her instructions to Godwyn. "No." Her voice was insistent.

Even the beast paused. Air rushed into Evie's lungs, and she used every bit of strength she could muster for one last burst of her gift. Now, instead of trying to send the void and the touch of her gift into the beast, she sucked it and his life force into herself.

Dark, unnatural life rushed into her, and she didn't just absorb it, she let it flow through her, and when she purged, she cast it from her. Not into this world but into the void. She didn't stop. She couldn't. The gift took over and refused even to slow itself once begun. There could be only one ending to this flow of power.

When it was completely destroyed and Evie came back to herself, she stood in the middle of the drawing room in Bethwood House. Hesta leaned against her back, and on the ground lay two bodies: a frozen, slime-covered Ekvard... and Godwyn.

Hesta fell to her knees to touch her brother, to check him for life, but Evie knew he was already dead. No one could withstand the touch of the demon and the void at the same time.

She stood beside Hesta and lay a comforting hand on her shoulder. Distraught, Hesta sobbed so hard her whole body shook, but all Evie could do was stand and be there. She couldn't shed a tear for Godwyn Bethwood, but no one deserved to have their body taken over by a demon like that.

"He needs a medic," Hesta said once her sobs allowed her to speak once more.

"It's too—"

"A medic, Evie."

"I'll go and get one."

30

E vie sat next to the stove and boiled pans of water. Some would be used to make tea, and the rest was for the medics who had come to look at Godwyn and Ekvard.

An inspector stood with her as she watched the pots. It was the same one who had visited before, and Inspector Willis had not been much use then, either.

"Let's go through what happened once more," he said. This time he had a notebook, and at least made a few notes.

"I told you before, and no matter how often you ask me, my story isn't going to change."

"Humour me."

"Godwyn and the other man were waiting for us when we came into the house. The other man, Ekvard, was one of the vitalists who came to the hospital to demonstrate his animal magnetism and mind control skills."

"But why would he come here?"

"I think Ekvard wanted to kill Hesta. He sounded really freaky, though. Was he on poppy juice or something?"

"We'll wait for that information from the medics," he said.

"I stood in front of Miss Bethwood, and first Ekvard tried to attack me, and then Godwyn tried to strangle me."

She pulled at her shirt, and around her neck a bruise had started to form. "Then they fell over. Dead-like."

"Just like that?"

"Yes, sir. Freaky, I'd say."

"I'd agree with you. It is most strange how two men could die with not a mark on either of them."

"You think we did something to them?"

"I do wonder," Willis said.

Evie made a fist and shook it at the inspector. "Even if I could hit one of them, do you think it's possible for me to do either of them any harm? And Miss Bethwood is only a little taller than I am. How could you even consider that we had anything to do with it?"

He stared at Evie and her hands, as though he were weighing up whether she could do anything untoward to two full grown men. "In this, I can't help but agree with you. I can't see how you two women could be any kind of threat to anyone." He scratched his head. "Unbelievable, really. How two healthy men could just fall down dead is beyond me."

"It's all beyond me, officer," she said. Although she knew exactly how they'd died. As she'd killed the beast, the beast had killed the men. She'd known that there was nothing she could do to save Ekvard, but she wasn't so sure about Godwyn. She might have been able to save him. Might.

"Well, thank you, Miss Chester. If we need anything more from you, I'll be in touch," the inspector said.

"Is Miss Bethwood free now? Is she all right? She looked distraught."

"She's with a constable and two medics. I think your idea of tea will be much welcome when she is done." He nodded to himself. "The medics will deal with those issues of health and so forth. Has Miss Bethwood made arrangements for her brother?"

"I'm not sure we even know what those are," Evie said.

"The medics will advise," he said. "However, she is in a

state of shock. She shouldn't be left alone. It might not be a good idea to stay here in this house either."

"I'll see to her care."

"Good," he said.

Evie stood at the stove and stared at the boiling water. Her thoughts danced and wouldn't stay at all still. When Hesta came into the room, Evie took one look at the tear-streaked face and eyes made red from crying, and she melted. No one needed to see their family die before their eyes. She put her arms around Hesta and guided her to a chair near the stove.

She made tea, sweetened it, added a little cold water to take the boiling heat from the drink, and pressed the cup into Hesta's hand.

"Drink," she said.

As bid, Hesta raised the cup to her lips and sipped. She paid no attention to the heat of the drink, and if she burned her lips, she said nothing.

"You can't stay here," Evie said.

Hesta looked up. "Why not?"

"You need to be away from here until... until everything is cleared away." She thought of the two bodies and the slime that had covered Ekvard.

"The medics are taking the remains away later. I have to be here."

"All right, and then we'll leave."

"Where will we go?"

"You're going to stay with me for a few days until the house is cleaned and you have had a chance to grieve."

Hesta stared at Evie, and her numbness seemed to break. The tears returned, and she wailed with such sorrow, Evie felt tears prickling in the corners of her eyes. Then Hesta's keening increased in pitch and volume so much, a glass on the shelf shattered and the covering of the carriage clock on the shelf split in two.

"Hesta," Evie said, "if you're not careful, you'll bring the house down."

The keening of Hesta's sorrow stopped, and she rushed into Evie's arms. Her tears flowed again, and Evie held her for a long time, until the tears and the sobs stopped.

"I'm fine," Hesta said, but she didn't pull away.

"You don't sound fine. The moment we can get away, we will."

When they'd shown up at Number 17 Ardmore Street and Agatha Hickman heard about what had happened, she welcomed Hesta into her house with the warmth due her own daughter instead of the sister of someone she neither liked nor trusted.

"I'll make you up a room," Agatha said. "It's small and basic, but it will suffice for a day or two. Or as long as you want to stay here."

Hesta reached out and touched Agatha's arm. "Can I stay with Evie?"

Agatha looked to Evie.

Evie shrugged. "If it helps."

"Please, Evie, I don't want to be alone. Not now. Not today."

When they retired for the evening, Hesta got into bed first and held out her hand. Evie glanced at Hesta once more before she turned away to finish her preparations for bed. This was more than just touching someone's hand. Now she had to be close.

"If you don't—" Hesta started as she slid to the edge of the bed, ready to leave.

"No," Evie finished. "It's fine. I'm just worried, in case I do anything embarrassing."

"Like what?"

"Sponging."

Hesta shook her head. "Doesn't matter."

"Probably not," Evie replied. She blew out the last candle

and slid under the covers next to Hesta. She lay still, like a rod of stiff and unbending iron.

"Hold me."

Evie took a moment before she reacted and then opened her arms so Hesta could lie against her.

"Never leave me, Evie," Hesta said. "I couldn't stand it. Not now."

"I'll never leave you. Now, sleep. You need to rest."

I hope you have enjoyed this story. If you did, please consider leaving an honest review. Most of all, I just want to know that you have enjoyed the story.

Thank you

If you want to know more about new books, background details and information not printed any place else, then subscribe to the reader's list.

https://www.subscribepage.com/nitaround

Visit my website at
www.nitaround.com

Or join my facebook group

www.facebook.com/groups/nitaroundbooks/

More Books in the Towers world

The Towers of the Earth

Prequel: A Pinch of Salt
Prequel: A Hint of Hope
Book 1: A Touch of Truth
Book 2: A Touch of Rage
Book 3: A Touch of Darkness
Book 4: A Touch of Ice

The Evie Chester Files:

Case 1: Lost and Found
Case 2: Sirens and Syphons
Case 3: Fur and Fangs

Printed in Great Britain
by Amazon

82755534R00120